DEAD IS THE NEW BLACK

marlene perez

HARCOURT, INC. Orlando Austin
New York San Diego London

Library of Congress Cataloging-in-Publication Data
Perez, Marlene.
Dead is the new black/Marlene Perez.
p.   cm.
Summary: While dealing with her first boyfriend and suddenly being pressed into
service as a substitute cheerleader, sixteen-year-old Daisy Giordano, daughter and sister
of psychics but herself a "normal," attempts to help her mother discover who is behind a
series of bizarre attacks on teenage girls in their little town of Nightshade, California.
[1. Supernatural—Fiction.   2. Cheerleading—Fiction.   3. Psychic ability—Fiction.
4. Interpersonal relations—Fiction.   5. High schools—Fiction.   6. Schools—Fiction.]
I. Title.
PZ7.P4258De   2008
[Fic]—dc22   2007027677
ISBN 978-0-15-207062-5 Scholastic edition

Text set in Adobe Jenson
Designed by April Ward

First edition
C E G H F D B

Printed in the United States of America

To my agent, Stephen Barbara, who got the party started

DEAD IS THE NEW BLACK

CHAPTER ONE

Being dead became fashionable approximately forty-five minutes after Samantha "the Divine" Devereaux came back from summer break.

Although stylish as ever, there was still something off about the Divine Devereaux. She strolled down the hall wearing a black top, a miniskirt, and stiletto heels. Her long blond hair had been freshly highlighted.

But unlike after previous summer vacations, Samantha didn't have that sun-kissed Cabo glow. Her skin was, forgive the phrase, dead white.

A large silver pendant hung around her neck, but I couldn't get a close look at it. I wasn't the only one trying to sneak a peek, because heads turned more than usual as she strutted down the hall.

"Get out of my way, Daisy," she snapped at me as she passed by.

She was only slightly hampered by the coffin she was dragging behind her. At first I thought it was a giant wheelie backpack.

But my clue came when Penny Edwards, who could have brought home a gold in social climbing if it were an Olympic sport, rushed up to Samantha. "Where *did* you get that . . ."

"Coffin," Samantha supplied helpfully. "Mort's Mortuary. Burnished mahogany. Scaled to size for those of us with petite frames." I could have sworn she eyed my thighs with a look of scorn.

"Lined with satin?" Penny asked.

She recoiled in horror. "Silk, of course."

"Of course," Penny tittered. Samantha went on her way, and Penny, faster than you could say dead girl walking, was on her cell phone to Mort's Mortuary.

After first period, I saw Mr. Amador, our principal, talking to Samantha in the hallway, so I loitered long enough to eavesdrop.

He started with a lot of throat clearing and then said, "My dear, why on earth have you adopted such an . . . unusual look? You look like a vampire."

"The preferred term is 'undead' or, if you must, 'living challenged,'" she said, nose in the air. "I'm *not* a vampire. The thought of drinking blood is disgusting. And think of all those calories!"

"But, but you're a student council member, head cheerleader. You represent Nightshade High to the world . . ."

"Now I represent Nightshade looking like this," Samantha said.

While Mr. Amador sputtered and coughed, she swept away

but called over her shoulder, "And why don't we let Daddy's lawyer decide whether or not I can continue to attend Nightshade High looking like this?" With that she snapped open her cell and punched in a number. Interesting that she had Daddy's lawyer on speed dial.

After Samantha lawyered up, Mr. Amador had no choice. He had to let Samantha wear whatever she wanted, as long as it was within the school dress code. And since our school dress code didn't say anything about dressing in black, dead white skin, or bloodred lips, he was stuck.

By the time the dismissal bell rang, I was sick of hearing everyone talking about Samantha's new "look." I shut my locker, which closed with a clang.

"Hey, Giordano, what's up?" Ryan Mendez asked. He was the closest friend I had these days. His dad was chief of police in Nightshade.

When I didn't answer but just stood there frowning, he continued, "I saw your mom on the news last night."

My mom had been helping his dad solve crimes since Ryan and I were both in diapers. Mom's a psychic, the real deal, not the kind who reads your palm for ten bucks. Although she could probably do that, too. Instead, she spends her time crime solving.

We live in a small town—peaceful enough, I guess, but it's always been a little strange here. Nightshade started as a little frontier town a couple of hundred years ago, and it had a long history of strange occurrences, odd inhabitants, and most of all, secrets. The town was full of secrets.

I realized I hadn't responded to Ryan. "Yep, Mom said as soon as she touched the scarf, she knew where the body was."

"Cool." Ryan turned to get a better view of Samantha giggling with Penny at her locker.

"What do you think about all that?" I murmured, with a nod toward Samantha.

"She still looks beautiful," he replied, not taking his eyes from her.

I restrained the involuntary gag that rose to my throat. He's had a crush on her since second grade.

I made a face.

"Daisy, I know you don't like her," Ryan continued. "And I know she embarrassed you back in middle school, but she didn't mean to."

Embarrass was an understatement. Humiliate. Devastate. Annihilate. Those were more accurate word choices.

"I don't want to talk about it," I said. "In fact, I'd be happy if her name was never mentioned again."

But Samantha Devereaux was all anybody wanted to talk about. The rest of the week was devoted to watching her every move and then rehashing it endlessly. The goths howled with rage and frustration: The popular kids, now sporting Samantha's look, were on their turf. Finally, in protest, the goths, girls and guys, switched to lime green or hot pink skirts, matching sweater sets, and pearls.

The one thing that people didn't seem to be able to duplicate was the pendant that never left Samantha's neck. I was curious about it, but since I wasn't in her close circle of friends, I still hadn't gotten a good look at it.

By Friday, I'd had more than enough of the Samantha Devereaux madness. After school, I sat on our porch swing with a glass of lemonade, trying to clear my head of the week's weirdness.

That's when I saw Samantha sitting on her boyfriend's Sean Walsh's front porch. She was using her coffin as a stool. Sean had lived next door to us since third grade, so I recognized his deep voice, a series of giggles from Samantha, and then silence.

Samantha Devereaux was dead and she had a better love life than me. Life wasn't fair.

My moment of solitude didn't last long anyway.

"It's your turn to cook dinner, twerp," my sister Poppy announced. She was only a year older than me, but she liked to push me around. Now that she was a senior, it was even worse.

She threw herself beside me on the swing, and it rocked violently.

"My lemonade!" I said, but it was too late. I watched as the glass started to tip over and then . . . didn't.

I looked up. Poppy smiled complacently.

"Show-off," I said. I headed for the kitchen.

Life wasn't fair. Poppy never used her telekinesis for anything major. I thought of all the things I would do if I had her powers. But I didn't, so it looked liked I'd be making dinner again the old-fashioned way.

Not only am I the baby, I'm the only nonpsychic in the family. My dad disappeared under mysterious circumstances when I was eleven. He was a normal just like me.

Do you know how hard it is to be the only nonpsychic in a family of psychics? Trust me, it's tough.

Like the time I had a date with Brian Miller (my first and *last* date, thanks to my sister Poppy.) I borrowed Poppy's sweater without asking, thinking she'd never find out. Her psychic abilities hadn't fully developed yet, so I figured I was safe.

But she knew all right.

When Poppy discovered her sweater was missing, she just concentrated and told it to come on home.

Unfortunately, I was with Brian at the time, sitting at the Dairy Queen. I was also wearing the sweater in question.

The date had been going well. He talked about himself—but not too much—and he had an adorable smile. The smiled faded fast when he saw my sweater hover in the air and then float out the door.

Luckily, I was wearing a cami under the sweater or it would have been even more embarrassing. As it was, Brian broke out in a sweat. He didn't even finish his sundae, and I was home twenty minutes later.

Needless to say, I never borrowed Poppy's clothes without asking again and Brian Miller never asked me on another date. And neither did anybody else.

It seemed like I was always the one who ended up cooking dinner. Mom's cases often kept her late. My other sister, Rose, who was a freshman at the local college, UC Nightshade, was always studying, and Poppy was—well, I don't know what Poppy was doing, besides annoying me. She certainly wasn't cooking dinner.

I rummaged through the contents of our fridge, which were pretty pathetic. Some wilted lettuce, a couple of cartons of suspicious-smelling takeout, and a twelve-pack of diet soda. I found some decent veggies in the keeper and some cheese. Not much to work with in the nutrition category. We needed to go grocery shopping again.

"I'll stop at the market after class tomorrow," Rose said, not even looking up from her books, which she hunched over at the kitchen table.

I hated it when she popped in and out of my mind without my consent. I knew she didn't mean to do it, but I didn't have to like it. There were certain things that were meant to stay private. Like certain thoughts about Ryan Mendez.

"Sorry," she added. "I know you hate it. I was thinking of something else and accidentally wandered in."

At least Rose tried to respect my privacy. "No, I'm just in a bad mood," I said. "Thanks for taking on the shopping."

I took the vegetables I'd found out of the fridge: tomatoes, mushrooms, and an iffy onion. I washed the tomatoes and set them aside, then I chopped the onion and mushrooms to sauté with a little garlic. I found a package of noodles and took out the bag of preshredded cheese. Lasagna it was.

"Hey, watch it!" Rose said. "You're getting tomato all over my notebook."

"But I'm not chopping tomatoes," I said. When I looked over, though, there was one exploded tomato on the counter.

"Poppy, knock it off or I swear—oh, hi, Mom," I said. "You're home early."

She stood in the doorway with her briefcase still in her hands. My mom was beautiful, even rumpled after a hard day at the office. Her long hair was midnight black and shiny, as though a cluster of stars shone in the strands.

My hair was the same basic color as hers, but on me it just looked dirty. Mom's eyes have been compared to sapphires. My eyes are more like the color of Windex.

"Rough day," Mom said. "How was yours?"

"Same as yours," I said. "Rough."

Mom smiled in sympathy. "Do you need any help with dinner?" she asked.

"Thanks, but I've got it under control."

"Thanks for cooking tonight. I don't think I could face making dinner after the day I had." She collapsed into a kitchen chair.

I looked at my mother curiously. She loved her work and rarely complained about it. She looked pale, and there were dark circles under her eyes.

I put the kettle on and made Mom a cup of tea. She sat at the counter and kept me company while I finished dinner.

After the lasagna was done and Poppy grudgingly set the table, we ate in the dining room.

"Daisy, this is delicious," Mom said.

"I used Grandma's recipe, with a few minor alterations."

I may not have psychic talents, but I make a mean lasagna.

After dinner, Rose and Poppy headed for the kitchen for clean-up duty. Mom headed for the living room. A few minutes later, I heard her talking on the phone.

I wandered in to read on the couch. Mom had a thick file in front of her. After a short conversation, she hung up the phone with an angry click. "That man is going to give me gray hair," she said.

"What man? And why?"

"The county coroner, Bud Larson. Because he's an idiot," she burst out. Then she sighed and said, "Forget I said that, Daisy. I'm frustrated and I'm taking it out on him."

I was quiet, hoping she would say more.

"He refuses to believe that my contributions are real, which means he doesn't spend any time on any of the cases I consult on."

"But that's not fair," I protested. No matter what, I knew my mom was right. She never made a mistake about her psychic readings.

"No, it's not," she agreed, "but fortunately, Nightshade's chief of police believes that my contributions are worth risking the wrath of the coroner's office."

"Chief Mendez is right," I said loyally. "You've helped so many people."

"But people like Bud Larson are afraid of the unknown, and psychics are part of that unknown."

Poppy and Rose came in while we were talking. They carried a large dessert tray.

"We thought we could have dessert in here," Rose said.

Mom nodded. "Poppy, why don't you get the TV trays. Daisy, this looks great." She held up a dish of ice cream and strawberries.

"Poppy must have made it." I'd forgotten about dessert, and ice cream was Poppy's favorite.

There was silence in the room while we all dug in.

"Rose," my mom said, "do you have a minute to take a look at something?"

"Sure," Rose said, popping a strawberry into her mouth. "What is it?"

Mom took a deep breath. "I might as well tell you all. I need help with a case."

Stunned silence. Mom never, ever needed help with a case.

"You never ask for help," Poppy said, tactful as usual.

"There's a file I want Rose to see. I can't get a reading on the body." My sisters and I searched Mom's troubled face. She continued, "The female victim was an unidentified young, healthy girl who seemed to just drop dead, and I can't determine why."

"Are you losing your psychic abilities?" Poppy blurted it out. "Are you becoming a—norm?"

The horror in her voice irritated me. I don't know what the big deal was. Being a "norm" wasn't so bad.

"You've had tough cases before," I reminded her. "Like that guy in Sydney, remember? Turned out he was bitten by a spider and the bite was so small that you barely got anything."

"This is different," Mom replied. "I sensed violence— someone taking something she didn't want to give, but there wasn't any sign of an injury. It's like someone just drained her of her life force. The coroner's office is stumped."

"Tell us what you know about the victim," I suggested.

"Not much, I'm afraid," Mom said. "A female approximately fifteen to seventeen years old. The police think she was a runaway. No signs of physical trauma. But I can't even get a glimpse of a childhood memory. It's like every thought, every feeling she had was erased."

"Why can't I help?" The question burst out of me.

"If she gets to, I'm helping, too," Poppy said.

"I don't think so, Daisy." Mom shook her head. Firmly.

Poppy gave a triumphant crow, and Mom turned to her with

a frown. "You either. I wouldn't have asked Rose, but she's the oldest and most experienced."

"But I want to help," I said.

"I know you do, honey," Mom said. "But I need Rose's help now."

"You mean Rose's psychic abilities," I said. I pushed away my dessert, suddenly no longer hungry. Resentment had a way of filling up your stomach. "May I be excused?"

Without waiting for an answer, I stomped off to my room. Not the most mature reaction, I admit, but I couldn't help it. I was so sick of Rose and Poppy having a part of Mom's life. A part I couldn't share. I knew I'd be able to help her with this case, if she'd just let me.

I had lots of detective-like skills, such as the ability to tell if someone was lying. Having an ex-friend like Samantha Devereaux had taught me that lesson.

After pouting for a few minutes, I had an idea. As I tiptoed downstairs, I heard my name.

"It's hard for Daisy," Mom said. "You girls need to try to include her more in your activities."

"There's so much she doesn't understand," Poppy said. "She's a *norm*, Mom. It's time you admit it."

"She's a late bloomer," Mom said. "You'll see. But normal or not, she's still your sister, and I expect you to treat her as such."

I forgot that the bottom step creaked and put my weight on it. The sound gave me away.

"Daisy, is that you?" Mom called from the family room.

"Yes, it's me," I said, pretending that I hadn't heard anything. I stepped into the family room. Poppy was sprawled on the couch and Mom and Rose were on either side of her. A cozy circle. A circle that excluded me.

I made a face. "I just want the cordless to call Ryan."

"Wow, Daisy, I didn't know you had it in you," Poppy said. "He *is* a hottie, but maybe a little out of your league."

"He's my *friend*, remember, Poppy? Don't be disgusting," I said. "Can I have the cordless?"

"Friend, huh? That may have been true when you were both playing in the sandbox, but if you haven't noticed, Ryan is all grown up now."

She crowed even louder when she saw the blush spread across my face. "I knew it! You do have a thing for him."

Too embarrassed to reply, I just held out my hand for the phone. Poppy usually carried the phone around like it was her security blanket. She reached under a pillow and handed it to me.

I stomped up the stairs. Poppy was such a pain in the butt sometimes. Even if I was interested in Ryan, I didn't have a chance. Not with Samantha Devereaux in existence.

I shut my bedroom door and locked it. Poppy's talents didn't include psychic eavesdropping, and Rose would never stoop so low, but there was still the garden variety of eavesdropping, like loitering outside the door to listen.

This was something I definitely didn't want my sisters to hear.

I took a deep breath and dialed Ryan's number. It was just Ryan, who I'd known all my life. Ryan, who'd shot up a foot the summer before high school. Ryan, with his green eyes and dark brown hair, hair that looked so soft I wanted to touch it.

"Mendez residence, Ryan speaking." Ryan's dad insisted he answer the phone that way. You know, the polite way.

There was a lump in my throat, which blocked my power of speech. Damn that Poppy! She had to open her big mouth and make me think about Ryan in that way.

"Hello?" Ryan said. "Daisy?"

Caller ID. Sometimes I hated technology. Like now, when it would have been so easy just to hang up.

"Hey, Ryan," I said finally.

"What's up?"

I'd called Ryan lots of times, but this was different because I needed a favor. A big one.

"Can you meet me tonight?" I asked.

"Uh, sure. Where?" Ryan's voice sounded resigned, not exactly the reaction I wanted from the hottest guy in school. I reminded myself I had no interest in Ryan Mendez.

"At the diner at around ten thirty." Slim's Diner was conveniently located across from the police station.

"Daisy, my curfew is midnight." Ryan's dad was strict, being the police chief and all.

"I know, I know. It won't take long."

"Okay," he said. "Do I want to ask what you're getting me into this time?"

"It's no biggie," I said, "but bring that extra set of keys. You know the ones." We both knew his dad kept a spare set of office keys at the house.

He groaned in exasperation, but he didn't say no.

CHAPTER TWO

Ryan was late. I checked my watch again. Definitely late.

I was the only one left in the place. Flo (her name really was Flo) came over and asked me pointedly, "Can I get you anything else?" Which was restaurant code for "You're the only one left in the place, so quit nursing that Sprite and skedaddle."

"Slow night?" I asked, hoping that conversation would distract her.

"The tips have been lousy," she groused. "And my feet are killing me."

Flo talked like some world-weary waitress from the fifties, the kind who showed up on late-night television musicals, but she was only twenty, hard-bodied, and with serious tats. And if you had asked her to wear a pink uniform and scarf, she would have shoved it down your throat. She wore jeans to work, along with one of her unending supply of T-shirts with slogans. This one said "SARCASM: JUST ONE OF THE MANY SERVICES WE PROVIDE."

I was afraid virginity would be a permanent state, in my case.

"I'm waiting for someone," I said. "He should be here any minute."

A second later, loud music filled the room. We both jumped.

"New jukebox," Flo explained. "It's a little touchy. It plays what it wants to."

I stared at her. We were the only two people in the place. "Who put the money in?"

The song playing was "Here Comes Your Man" by the Pixies.

Flo shrugged. "Nobody. It's just different from other jukeboxes. Slim called someone to come out and fix it and everything. He couldn't find a thing wrong with it."

Flo glanced over my shoulder at someone who was coming into the diner and gave a sparkling smile. You didn't have to be a psychic to know it was Ryan.

"It's about time," I said, without turning around. Flo only smiled like that for Ryan.

He sat down across from me. "How'd you know it was me?"

"I have my ways." I smirked.

"Sorry I'm late. I had something to take care of." He turned to Flo. "Can I have a cup of coffee? Whatever's in the pot is fine."

"That swill? Don't be silly," Flo said. "I'll make you a fresh pot."

Flo didn't use words like *silly*. It sounded so girlish, so flirtatious. So not Flo. Ryan did seem to have that effect on the opposite sex.

I frowned and looked at the clock again. "You'd better get

your coffee to go," I told him. I wanted to make sure we had plenty of time to investigate.

"Daisy, are you sure this is a good idea?"

"Of course I'm sure," I said. I ignored the fact that if Mom found out, I'd probably be grounded until graduation. Mine, not Poppy's.

After Ryan paid the check and Flo handed him a huge cup of coffee to go, we were finally ready.

"Did you remember the keys?" I asked him once we were outside.

He nodded. "What do you need them for this time?"

"The morgue." I didn't look at him when I said it.

"New hobby?"

"I need to look at a dead body."

"Of course you do," he said. "What else would you do in the morgue?" He took my arm as we crossed the street. "Well, we'd better hurry. Officer Denton is about to take his nightly cigarette break."

I wondered briefly how Ryan knew so much about Officer Denton's habits, but the feel of his hand on my arm distracted me.

Main Street was empty of people. There weren't even any cars in sight, except the lone police cruiser parked in front of the station.

Ryan looked up and down the street. "We really need to get a movie theater or something. It's like the town dies every night at eight."

We weren't really going to the *actual* morgue. The nearest real morgue was in Santa Cruz, but "the cooler," as I'd heard Chief Mendez call it, was the place where bodies could be temporarily stored in Nightshade. This body would probably be shipped off to Santa Cruz before the weekend was over, so we had to act fast.

As we neared the side door, the sound of Officer Denton's voice carried in the night air. "But honey, I think we should wait until . . ."

His voice faded, but I could tell he was pacing outside as he talked on the phone with Tammy Clarkson, his girlfriend of twelve years. Everyone in town had a pool about when he was going to pop the question. I had a five spot on Valentine's Day 2020, but I'm a romantic.

Ryan rummaged in his pocket and withdrew a set of keys. When he handed them to me, I fit the key in the lock. The door opened with a groan. We froze, but we could still hear Officer Denton talking on his cell.

"If my dad catches us—"

"He won't," I promised rashly. "We'll only be a few minutes."

Once we were inside, it took me a few minutes to get my courage up. I flicked on the pen-sized flashlight I'd brought and shone it around the room.

There was a beat-up metal desk and a filing cabinet in one corner. The remainder of the room was taken up by a long table, and along the other wall, a row of refrigerated steel drawers.

The cooler was not the place to stash a cold soda. The cooler was the place to stash a dead body. I gulped.

"Are you sure you want to do this?" Ryan asked. His voice sounded soft, concerned. His hand brushed mine, and every molecule in my body jumped to meet him.

"I have to do this," I replied after a minute. "Mom needs my help. She just doesn't know it yet. Can you guard the door?"

Ryan went off to play lookout while I did some snooping.

All the talk at school about vampires had me spooked, but I took a deep breath and approached the cooler.

A gust of cold air slammed the breath from my body when I opened the first compartment. To my relief, it was empty. I knew I didn't have much time for snooping, but I'd never seen a dead body before and it wasn't something I was looking forward to. I shivered and breathed in through my mouth. There was a strong chemical smell in the room, but it couldn't completely disguise another, more unpleasant odor. I steeled myself not to think about it and opened another drawer.

There she was—a shell that used to be a person.

I could tell she'd probably been attractive when she was alive—red hair, petite figure. Her shoulders were bare and she looked cold, draped in a white sheet. I resisted the urge to put my jacket around her thin shoulders. I checked her neck, looking for fang marks. I felt a little ridiculous doing it, but anything was possible in Nightshade. Her neck was long and white, but it didn't have a mark on it.

I didn't know what I was doing. Why had I tried to help? This death stuff was way beyond my abilities. I wasn't psychic. I wasn't a detective. What I knew about solving mysteries could be found in the pages of a Nancy Drew novel.

On her right hand was a smudged ink stamp. I could just make out the word *Opal*.

Could Opal be her name? But why would she stamp her own name on her hand?

There was a tattoo of a four-leaf clover on the base of her left thumb. That lucky charm hadn't brought her much luck. I also noticed that her long auburn hair had a thick white streak that extended along the part, all the way down to the tip of her hair.

I moved away from the body. There wasn't anything I could do for her now, except try to find her killer.

Then, out of the corner of my eye, I thought I saw a movement. I held still, barely daring to breathe, and watched. There it was again. Her hand moved, I was sure of it.

"Is there anybody there?" I said, and then felt foolish when I remembered what Mom had told me, that bodies sometimes gave the illusion of movement after death.

Just my imagination. I closed the drawer containing the body and clicked off my flashlight. I had a few clues but didn't know what to do with them.

Ryan burst into the room. "We've got to leave now!" he panted. He moved closer, until he practically bumped into me, then handed the keys to me. "Hold on to these."

I heard footsteps coming closer. I couldn't see his face in the dark, but I knew his face mirrored the panic welling up inside me.

"Officer Denton," I hissed. "What do we do?"

Ryan grabbed my hand. "I have an idea," he said. "Just play along, okay?" His palms were sweaty.

The footsteps sounded like they were right outside the door. Ryan drew me closer.

"Wha . . . ?"

That's when Ryan kissed me. It was obvious he'd had lots of practice. I hadn't, but I was a quick learner.

I liked the way he cradled my cheeks in his hands as we kissed.

He pressed his body closer to mine. I moved backward until my butt touched something cold. He'd backed me into the cooler. The thought repulsed me for a second and I tried to shove him away.

"Kiss me back," he whispered, and I responded, all thoughts of where we were flying out of my brain. I wriggled closer and touched my lips to his once again. His hands tangled in my hair and his lips met mine.

We heard a loud throat-clearing, and then someone turned on the light switch. Ryan and I stood blinking in the sudden brightness. I realized I was still in his arms and took a giant step backward like we were playing a game of hokey-pokey, rather than a game of hanky-panky.

"Mendez," Officer Denton said, "what did I tell you would happen if I caught you in here with a girl again?"

"You'd call my dad," Ryan replied glumly.

A girl? My brain registered. *Again?* Who had Ryan brou
to the morgue? And why the morgue?

Officer Denton stared at us for a few seconds. "I thought I
took your keys away last time," he said.

"The door was already open when I came in," Ryan said.
Technically not a lie, since I was the one who opened it.

I found my voice. "Please don't call his father. I asked Ryan to
bring me here. It's not his fault."

Officer Denton could barely restrain himself from giving
Ryan a congratulatory high five.

I glared at Ryan. It'd probably be all over the county tomorrow about what a stud the Mendez kid was. If it wasn't already, I
thought, remembering Officer Denton's words, particularly the
part about the *girl* and *again*.

Finally, we convinced Officer Denton not to say anything to
Ryan's dad or my mom. After giving us a stern warning to head
straight home, Officer Denton let us off the hook.

Ryan insisted on walking me home, even though it was almost his curfew. I stared straight ahead the whole time. It took us
about ten minutes to get from the station to my house at the
other end of town—and people think I'm exaggerating about
how small Nightshade is.

We were in front of my house. I opened the gate and we
started up the walkway.

Ryan stopped in his tracks. "Daisy, I'm really sorry about that
kiss," he said.

and looked at him. "Thanks a lot," I said.

mean it that way," he said. "I just meant that a

he best place for a first kiss."

ound like it was a first for *you*," I said.

Ryan said softly, "Daisy—"

"You're going to miss your curfew," I said.

He didn't budge.

"It's no big deal," I said.

"You seem mad," he said, leaning against the fence.

"I'm not mad," I said, gritting my teeth and smiling as pleasantly as possible. "You just took me by surprise, that's all. Next time, just give me a little notice."

"A little notice before I kiss you?" Ryan said. He grinned widely. "I can do that. I'm going to . . ."

He leaned in. I never found out what he was going to do, because the porch light flickered on.

I saw a curtain stir at one of the front windows. I was going to kill Poppy.

"I'll see you later," Ryan said. I watched him as he hopped our low picket fence and took off, whistling in the dark. Why was he in such a good mood?

I was in a pretty good mood myself, I thought, remembering the kiss. What was I thinking? Ryan Mendez and me? As if I didn't have enough problems.

CHAPTER THREE

I glared at Ryan's back. He was in the front, right next to the volleyball net. Rachel King, who was on the opposite team, was halfheartedly checking him out.

Rachel was on the cheerleading squad with Samantha Devereaux. I'd always liked her the best out of all the cheer clones. She was probably the second most gorgeous girl at Nightshade High—second only to Samantha.

Rachel had long curly brown hair, smooth skin the color of an iced latte, and deep blue eyes. She didn't look gorgeous today, however. Her skin had a green cast to it, like the algae that grew in Poppy's fish tank. It looked like she'd tried a home highlighting kit, and the effect was startling: there was a long white streak in her hair.

I glared at Ryan again. It was already Wednesday and he hadn't said any more about our kiss in the morgue. In fact, he hadn't said much of anything. He seemed to have urgent business on the other side of the galaxy whenever I appeared.

What was his damage? It was just a kiss between friends. It

was no big deal. That's what I tried to tell myself, but it was more than a big deal. It was the kind of kiss that poets write sonnets about, but Ryan Mendez was too stupid to see it. Or maybe he was on the receiving end of fabulous kisses every day of the week.

It was my turn to serve. Ryan turned to watch me and then looked away quickly. I hit the ball as hard as I could. It went right for Ryan's head, but he ducked at the last minute and it careened into the net.

"Sorry," I called, smiling sweetly.

Samantha Devereaux had managed to dye her P.E. uniform black. She still had the pendant on as well. I thought Ms. Foster was going to read her the riot act about her uniform when she pointed to Samantha and said, "Why are you wearing that in my P.E. class?"

Samantha tried to look innocent. "What do you mean?"

"Miss Devereaux, you are fully aware that I do not allow any jewelry to be worn in my gym. It's a safety hazard."

"I'm sorry," she said, smiling sweetly.

For a minute, I thought Ms. Foster would take the pendant from Samantha, but instead she blew her whistle again. Figures that Sam would get away without a demerit for a dress code infraction. The teachers at school let her get away with murder, just because she is the captain of the cheerleading squad.

The other team rotated, and it was Rachel's turn to serve. She stepped up to the line and then crumpled to the floor.

Ms. Foster blew her whistle as a crowd gathered around

Rachel as she lay on the floor. I stood in the back and hoped that she was okay.

"Step back, please," Ms. Foster said. "She needs a little room."

A minute later, Rachel sat up. "What happened?" she asked.

"You fainted," Ms. Foster said. "But I'm sure you're fine now."

"Shouldn't we take her to the nurse or something?" I asked. Ms. Foster was new, substituting for Mrs. Lamb, who was out on maternity leave, but weren't teachers supposed to know this kind of stuff?

"Yes, yes, of course," Ms. Foster said. "Daisy, could you and Ryan help Rachel to the nurse's office?"

Ryan didn't look at me as we each took one of Rachel's arms and helped her to her feet.

We kept our arms around her as we escorted her to the nurse's. I noticed that Rachel leaned heavily on Ryan's shoulder. She even fluttered her eyelashes, but weakly.

I knocked on the nurse's door. Nurse Phillips answered and then took over, *tsk*ing at the sight of Rachel's pasty complexion.

Nurse Phillips had a retro thing going. Cherry red lipstick, cat's-eye glasses, and platinum blond hair done up in a beehive do so high it blocked out the sun. She looked like someone ready to go to the hop, but I guesstimated her age to be somewhere in the midthirties.

I breathed in and almost choked on the smell of Aqua Net hairspray. Nurse Phillips's hairstyle probably required cases of the stuff.

"Let's get her on the cot," she said. Then to Rachel she added, "We'll have you right as rain in a minute. Leave it to me."

As Rachel lay there on the cot, I noticed the streak in her hair again. Had it somehow gotten even paler since we left the gym? Then I remembered that the girl in the morgue had a streak in her hair, too. Fad, or something freakier?

"Will she be okay?" I asked, but Nurse Phillips ignored the question.

"Thank you for bringing her to me," she said, "I'll take care of her now. Daisy, can you ask Ms. Meyers in the office to call Rachel's parents?"

I nodded. The big lump of worry in my throat wouldn't let me speak, but Nurse Phillips shooed us out into the hallway and shut the door firmly in our faces, blocking out Rachel's prone form.

Ryan and I stood there and examined the beige walls.

He cleared his throat. "Daisy, we need to talk," he said.

Typical. He wanted to talk now, of all times. "You heard Nurse Phillips. I have to go to the office."

"Later then?"

"Later." I went to the office, delivered my message, and then headed back to gym class.

The gym was empty. I checked the huge clock that hung on the wall opposite the double doors. The volleyball game had ended without me.

I wasn't heartbroken about it or anything. Gym was, thankfully, my last class of the day. I mean, who wants to go through the day with sweat sticking to their clothes? Or worse yet, get naked and take a shower with twenty of your classmates?

Mandatory showers had been dropped in the fall, when Lilah Porter protested the archaic practice by staging a sit-in in the gym, where she set up a projector and played the shower scene from *Carrie* in a continuous loop until the school board caved.

I headed for the locker room to change. I wondered what Ryan wanted to talk about. The kiss, probably. The thought made me squirm. I hoped he didn't think I'd get all clingy and that he'd have to let me down gently.

I'd tell him the kiss meant nothing, I decided. Absolutely nothing.

Still, I didn't want to dwell on the question of who else Ryan had kissed in the morgue. But however much I tried, I couldn't stop thinking about it. Which is why I wasn't quick enough to avoid Ms. Foster.

I was walking into the girls' locker room when she found me. She wore designer sweats in white with red trim. Nightshade High School colors.

"Daisy," she said. "I was so looking forward to a chat with you."

"Me?" What did Miss Foster want to talk to me about? Then I realized she'd want to know how Rachel was doing.

"We left her with Nurse Phillips," I said. "Her parents are on the way."

"Who?" She stared at me.

I stared back. She couldn't have forgotten about Rachel already. It wasn't every day that someone fainted in gym class, although some people had tried faking it.

"Oh, yes, the Davis girl."

"Rachel *King*," I prompted. "Ms. Foster, don't you remember?"

"Yes, yes, I'm sure she'll be fine," she replied, "And it's *Miss* Foster, not *Ms*. Gotta let them know you're available, and a silly ol' *Ms*. won't do that, now will it?"

Miss Foster? It sounded so last century. I didn't think anybody used that term anymore, except Miss McBennett at the post office, and she had to be eighty.

She studied my troubled face. "You mustn't worry. It causes wrinkles," she said.

Her face was pink and smooth as a baby's. Clearly, Ms.—I mean *Miss*—Foster didn't worry much.

There was a gleam in her eye that I recognized. I'd seen ladies at the skin-care counter at Nordstrom with that exact same look. Two-hundred-dollar face cream, I guessed.

"You probably know that not only am I the physical education coach, I am also the cheerleading coach," she continued. "I can tell that you are physically fit."

"I guess," I said. She was looking me up and down so thoroughly that I knew she could probably guess my weight to the nearest ounce.

I was glad I'd given up chocolate. Not really, but it sounds better than the truth, which is that I had been jonesing for chocolate the way Poppy longed for unlimited cell minutes. My habit was so bad that I finally put a stop to it after I spent a week's worth of lunch money on some imported Swiss dark chocolate, 92 percent pure.

I'd lost track of what Miss Foster was saying. Chocolate will do that.

What she said then shocked me so much that I made her repeat it. "You want me to do *what?*"

"I want you to try out for the cheerleading team."

I was stunned. Me, a cheerleader?

"I don't think so," I said.

"Just think about it," Miss Foster said. "Cheerleader tryouts aren't for another week. With the Davis girl out sick, we're short. We have no choice but to replace her, and fast."

I didn't bother to try to correct her again about Rachel's last name. I was too busy trying to dodge trying out for cheerleading, but Miss Foster wouldn't leave until I promised I'd at least think about it. But deep down I knew that I didn't fit in with the cheerleaders. There was no way I was going to try out.

When she walked back to her office, I changed into my street clothes, stuffed my gym uniform back into my locker, and gathered up my stuff.

It had been a weird day and it was time to go home. Unfortunately, the weirdness wasn't over.

Ryan was waiting for me just outside the girls' locker room door, but far enough away that everyone wouldn't think he was a perv like Tommy Landis, who drilled a hole in the wall between the locker rooms. He got caught, eventually, but all the girls were really glad that Lilah Porter had already won the shower-after-gym battle.

"It's late," he said. "What did Ms. Foster want, anyway?"

"Apparently, it's *Miss* Foster and she wants me to try out for cheerleading."

Ryan snorted. "You, a cheerleader?"

"What's that supposed to mean? You don't think I'm good enough for the cheerleading squad?" My voice was climbing an octave or so.

"It's not that," he said. "You just don't seem like the type."

"But Samantha Devereaux *is* the type?"

"Well, yeah," Ryan said, "but—"

"But nothing. I've got news for you. I'm trying out and nothing you say can change my mind." What gave him the right to tell me I couldn't try out? I was just as good as Samantha any day of the week. I took tumbling with her in third grade, as a matter of fact. She had trouble with her cartwheels and was sloppy with her splits.

I whirled around and stomped outside.

I was going to try out, and I was going to make it. I was going to be the best damn cheerleader Nightshade High had ever seen.

CHAPTER FOUR

I didn't get very far. Ryan caught up with me by the old oak tree in front of the school.

"Daisy, wait up! I want to talk to you," Ryan called as he broke into a jog. I refused to look behind me again, but I could hear the sound of his footsteps as he came closer.

I forced myself not to run, even though I didn't want to have this conversation with Ryan. Not now. Not ever. Not the letting-her-down-gently bit.

I knew it by heart. I should, I'd helped him practice it enough times. Ryan was a nice guy. He didn't like to crush the hopes of some freshman who was locker-stalking him. So he had a prepared speech.

A speech I wasn't going to hear. Not today. In his defense, I knew Ryan had no clue about how I felt about him. Not until we kissed, that is. That may have given him a clue. I sped up.

His hand touched my shoulder. "Daisy?"

I whirled around. "I get it!"

He recoiled from the heat in my voice. "I didn't mean to hurt your feelings. I just wanted to talk to you about—"

"The kiss, I know. We're better off friends, yada yada."

He looked puzzled. "No, I wanted to talk to you about the girl we . . . visited the other night." And then, in case I didn't catch on, he added in a low voice, "At the morgue."

I stopped long enough to process what he had said. Relief coursed through me. I wasn't going to be subjected to a humiliating *It isn't you, it's me* speech. "What about her?"

"I may have some new information," Ryan said.

A clue. He had to be the cutest Hardy Boy ever, especially when he smiled at me like that.

"What did you find out?" I started walking again, but this time at a more reasonable pace.

Ryan fell into step beside me. "I heard my dad talking the other night."

"And?" I prompted him.

"She disappeared," he replied.

"Who?"

"The girl in the morgue. She's gone."

"What? When?"

"Saturday night. Something conked Denton on the head, and when he woke up, the morgue had been trashed and the body was gone."

"The body has been missing for four days now?" I yelped. "Why didn't you say something earlier?"

Ryan shrugged. "It seemed like you were avoiding me." He was actually blushing. Maybe I wasn't the only one who was insecure.

He leaned in until our shoulders touched. I caught my breath and took in his smell of freshly brewed coffee and dark chocolate. Two of my favorite fragrances. I turned my attention back to what he was saying.

"I think Dad knows something about the case. Something he's not telling anyone." He stepped out onto the empty street.

An image flashed in my mind, and I yanked him back onto the sidewalk. "Wait!" I said.

"What the . . . ?" But he never finished the sentence, because a dark gray hearse squealed around the corner and into the intersection. The driver peeled away, doing about sixty in a thirty-five-mile-an-hour speed zone.

"Thanks!" Ryan said. "That guy would have hit me if you hadn't stopped me. How did you know?"

I changed the subject because I didn't know how I knew. The image was in my mind, and a minute later it was happening.

"Was that Nicholas Bone driving?" The Bone family owned the town funeral home, Mort's Mortuary. Mort Bone was a nice man. When he wasn't supervising a viewing, he wore polo shirts and plaid pants and was most often spotted getting in eighteen holes at the town's golf course. But his son Nicholas was a different matter. Nicholas Bone was trouble. Gorgeous trouble, but trouble just the same.

"I heard he skipped town after graduation," Ryan said.

Nicholas had been in Rose's class at Nightshade High. He broke my sister's heart their junior year. Great. I didn't want to be the one to tell Rose he was back in town, although all things considered, she probably already knew.

We were a few blocks from my house, almost within Rose's unintentional mental eavesdropping zone. I tugged on Ryan's hand to stop him. Tingles shot up my fingers, my wrists, all the way to my heart. "Back to this disappearing body . . . ," I said.

A couple of kids from school were headed toward us. I dropped Ryan's hand before they spotted us.

We fell silent as they passed by. The freshman girl, Katie something, kept glancing back at us over her shoulder. Probably another member of the Ryan Mendez fan club.

After they were out of earshot, I said, "How does a body disappear without a trace? It can't just get up and walk away."

"It can't, not if it was anything human," His breath tickled my ear as he lowered his voice.

My mouth opened, guppylike, as I took in his meaning. Nightshade *was* an odd town.

"What did the body look like?" Ryan asked. "I never even got a chance to talk to you about it after we were busted by Officer Denton."

"She looked . . . dead," I said, shoving aside the memory of the twitching hand.

"Did you notice anything unusual?"

I almost snapped that I didn't spend as much time in the morgue as he did, so I didn't know what was usual for a dead body, but then I looked into his gorgeous green eyes and stopped myself. "She had a tattoo on her left hand and a stamp on her right. The stamp said 'Opal.' Do you think that's her name?"

Ryan's eyes widened. "Was it a purple stamp?"

I nodded.

"That's probably from the Black Opal," he said.

I had no idea what he was talking about. "The what?"

"The Black Opal. It's a club in Santa Cruz."

"Oh," I said, feeling totally uncool for not knowing. "You've been there?"

Ryan nodded. "A bunch of us were there last weekend."

As well as I knew him, it was easy to forget that Ryan had a whole other, more popular group of friends. The kind of friends who went to clubs in Santa Cruz on the weekends instead of sitting at home trying out new recipes.

"I guess I'll just have to check it out for myself," I said.

"Daisy, I want you to promise me you won't go there alone."

I looked him in the eye. "I can't promise you that," I said as we approached my house, "but I will promise you that I'll let someone know where I'm going. *If* I go," I added, just so he didn't think he knew me like the back of his hand or anything.

Ryan raised his eyebrow and stared at me. We both knew I

would be in that club before he could say "VIP room." "So, tomorrow night, then?" he offered.

"Thanks, Ryan," I said. "You don't know how much I appreciate this."

"I'd do anything for you, Daisy," he said softly. "Just ask."

The intensity in his eyes unnerved me. My knees were trembling so badly I had to grab on to our picket fence for support.

"This is me," I said inanely, pushing open the gate. Like Ryan hadn't been to my house a million times. He had, but this time was different.

Very different, I realized, when Ryan reached over and gave me a peck on the lips. Quick, but tasty. The fast food of kisses.

"I'll call you later," he said, then jogged away.

I practically floated up the walkway to the house. Ryan kissed me. Again. He was going to call me.

Wait. *Why* was Ryan going to call me? To ask me out or to talk about the case? It was a mystery to me. As I climbed the porch steps, my euphoria deflated. I kicked the door in frustration. Just a little kick, but Poppy busted me.

"You know Mom hates it when you do that," she said.

"Oh, go psy yourself," I said.

"Jeesh, you're in a bad mood," Poppy said.

I walked away from her, into the kitchen, but she followed me.

"I don't understand why, especially since Ryan walked you home and gave you that sweet little kiss on the lips."

"Don't you have anything better to do than spy on me?" I snapped.

"No, not really," Poppy admitted cheerfully.

I went from wanting to strangle her to bursting into laughter in ten seconds flat.

Poppy giggled along with me and then went to the fridge and poured a couple of glasses of milk. She peered into the fridge. "I'm hungry and there's nothing to eat."

"Rose still hasn't done the grocery shopping," I said.

"She's been really absentminded lately," Poppy commented.

"I hadn't noticed," I said. I had, but I wasn't going to tell Poppy. She'd just use it as ammo the next time she and Rose got in a tiff. They always made up, but then they somehow always ended up mad at me.

"Where's Mom?" I asked.

"She called earlier and said she's working on a case with Chief Mendez. She said they'd grab something out," Poppy told me. "Oh, and I forgot to mention. Samantha Devereaux called."

"She called *here*?" My incredulity was clear. She really must be dead, because that was the only way she'd get caught calling me.

"I thought you were friends," Poppy said.

"No, we're not friends," I said shortly.

"But you were," Poppy persisted. "She used to be here all the time."

"Yeah, back in sixth grade." I took a gulp of milk. "When I didn't know any better," I added under my breath.

"She left her number." Poppy handed me a slip of paper. "She said it was urgent."

What did the queen of the dead want now? Whatever it was, I'm sure it involved plenty of pain and humiliation. For me, of course.

CHAPTER FIVE

I *forgot* about Samantha's call until after dinner, when I went upstairs to tackle my homework. I decided not to call Her Deadness back. Whatever it was, it could wait until school tomorrow. Unlike the rest of the student body, I wasn't going to jump when she snapped her fingers.

Bad decision.

The next day, I was at my locker right before lunch when Samantha strode up, wheeling her backpack-slash-minicoffin behind her.

"Tryouts are in five minutes," she said. Her cheerleading uniform had been dyed black and she wore blood red ribbons in her hair.

I raised an eyebrow. "New school colors?"

"Principal Amador gave me permission," she said. "Not that it's any of your business."

Then the part about tryouts sunk in. My stomach took the express elevator to my knees, which began to shake.

"But it's lunchtime," I whined. "And nobody told me tryouts were today. Ms., I mean Miss, Foster said they'd be next week."

"Cheerleaders don't eat lunch," she said. "And plans change. Rachel King is in the hospital and two other girls on the squad just came down with mono or something."

"Rachel's in the hospital?"

"That's what I said," she snapped.

I glared at her. "What's the matter with her?"

Her expression thawed. "They don't know what's wrong yet, but she won't be back in time for regionals. Miss Foster is flipping out. She's insisting we have three alternates instead of just one."

"Who else is sick?"

"Mindy Monson and Kelsey Sebastian. Kelsey and Mindy can't even have visitors. Now quit stalling. Let's go." She started to walk away.

I didn't follow her. My brain was too busy processing all the information she'd given me. It worried me that so many girls on the squad were ill.

I felt a little ill myself at the thought of cheerleader tryouts. Samantha whirled around and walked back to where I stood rooted to the spot.

"Let's go," she repeated.

"I can't," I said. "I didn't have time to practice."

"Well, you would have if you had called me back yesterday." She softened when she saw my face. "Don't look so scared. Look, I know we haven't been the best of friends or anything lately."

Or anything? What a vast understatement.

"The team needs you," Samantha continued. "You don't think I remember, but I do. You were a gymnast, a good one."

My gymnastics career ended early, when an enormous growth spurt put me out of the running. Good gymnasts weren't tall, at least not any I knew.

Now the only gymnastics I did was when Poppy "accidentally" locked me out of the house and I had to climb up the trellis to my bedroom window to get in.

"I'm out of practice," I said. "And I don't want to try out in front of a bunch of people." The football players often sat in on cheering tryouts. What if Ryan saw me? I'd be a nervous wreck.

"Miss Foster convinced Principal Amador that this was an emergency situation," Samantha said. "It's a closed tryout." She gave me a knowing look. "Ryan Mendez won't be judging your cartwheels today."

"What is that supposed to mean?"

"It's all over school," she said, but then glanced at her watch. "We're late."

"What's all over school?" I asked.

But she ignored the question and instead grabbed my arm and pointed me toward the gym. "Go change. You have about thirty seconds."

I found myself running toward the gym.

"It'll be fun," she hollered after me. "You'll see. We're a nice group of girls, if you get to know us."

The problem was, I did know Samantha, at least I thought I did. And I didn't trust her one little bit. Her words had been comforting, though, and unlocked the paralyzing fright that had washed over me at the thought of deliberately drawing attention to myself.

I threw on my P.E. uniform, which was wrinkled and slightly pungent. I thanked my lucky stars that Ryan wouldn't be seeing this debacle.

Then a thought occurred to me. What if Samantha was setting me up? Call me paranoid, but it wouldn't be the first time she'd punked me. What if I tried out and it was just some big joke? Miss Foster had talked to me about joining, but that didn't mean this tryout was real.

So I tiptoed down the hall and opened the gym door just a crack.

Samantha had been telling the truth. No letter jackets in sight. Miss Foster, Mr. Amador, and what was left of the cheer squad were sitting at a long table. In front of them was a row of girls, most of whom looked as scared as I felt.

I slipped in next to Penny Edwards, who gave me a confident smile, then gave the thumbs-up to Samantha, who ignored her. Penny wore black from the top of her dyed hair to the Chucks she wore on her feet. She also rattled a little when she moved. I squinted and noticed what looked like chicken bones in her hair. At least I *hoped* they were chicken bones. The rest of the girls were wearing designer sweats or butt cuts and silky camisoles (mostly in black, the color of choice these days), outfits to enhance their attractiveness. I looked like I was wearing gym clothes that had been in my locker for two weeks, which I was.

I stood there for the next half hour while Samantha called out names. She consulted her clipboard officially, which was bogus, because Nightshade High was a small school. There were only a hundred people in our class. I'd bet money she knew the name and probably the grade point average of every girl standing there.

I stretched while the other girls tried out. She finally called my name. Last, of course. I had pent-up energy to burn, so I started out with a couple of round offs and then went into a midair toe touch. I ended with a split. My muscles protested a little, but I ignored them. I stood up to show them what else I had (not much), when Miss Foster stopped me.

"Thank you, Daisy," she said. "I believe we've seen enough."

Samantha added, "Thank you all for coming. The results will be posted today after school."

I stood there and fumed. It had to be a joke. I'd barely had the chance to warm up before my tryout was over. I waited until everyone else had left and then walked over to Samantha.

"Thanks a lot," I said. "Why even bother having me try out? You knew I was nervous and you made me go last."

My voice sounded whiny, even to my own ears, but Samantha answered me patiently. "I had you try out because you're the best we've got. And I made you go last because it wouldn't be fair to the other girls if I hadn't. Some of *them* haven't had eight years

45

of gymnastics, Daisy. If I had let you go first, it would have intimidated girls like Penny, who never even took basic tumbling."

"Oh, okay," I said, feeling a tiny bit ashamed for snapping at her.

My stomach growled loudly. Samantha stared at me.

"I know, I know. Cheerleaders don't eat lunch."

She bent down and rifled through her coffin. My eye was drawn to the necklace she'd worn ever since she came back from summer vacation a changed girl. It looked old—ancient even. The silver was slightly tarnished, but I could make out some sort of symbol in the middle of the pendant.

She came back up with a couple of granola bars. I quickly averted my eyes from her necklace. She didn't seem to notice my interest.

Instead, she handed me one of the bars. "Cheerleaders are prepared for any emergency. We can't have you fainting in class."

"Thanks," I said, surprised.

Now that I was alone with Sam, I finally got up the nerve to ask her something I'd been wondering about for a while. "What's up with all the black clothes?"

"Since when are you the fashion police?" she snapped. "I can dress however I want, Daisy."

"I know, but it's just so different from the way you used to look," I said. "Did anything happen this summer that brought on the change?"

For a brief moment, Samantha looked vulnerable, almost like the girl who I used to call my friend, but in an instant, her mask of cool was back. "No," she said. "I just wanted a change, okay?"

"And the pendant?" Now that I was up close and personal with Her Deadness, I could finally get a good look at the symbol on it. "Is that an ankh?" All I knew about the ankh symbol was that it was Egyptian. And that was only because we studied Egypt in seventh grade.

"Yes," she answered, now beyond testy. "God, Daisy, what's with all the questions? I don't have time for this." And with that, she stormed off, her coffin trailing behind her.

"See you later," I called.

"Yes, you will," she replied. I wasn't sure if that was good news or bad news.

After school, I spotted Ryan hanging out by my locker. He was deep in conversation with Samantha's boyfriend, Sean.

The sight of Ryan set my heart thumping. I watched him out of the corner of my eye while I grabbed the books I'd need for homework later.

He broke off his conversation and hurried over. "Hey, Daisy, where have you been? I looked for you in the cafeteria at lunch."

I turned to speak to him, leaving my locker door open.

"What do you want, Ryan?" Despite my best efforts to control it, my voice was noticeably cool.

"Sean, Samantha, and I want to take you out tonight," he said.

I whirled around, furious. I didn't need a consolation dinner. It was bad enough that Ryan didn't think I was the cheerleader type. There was no need to rub my abysmal tryout in my face.

My locker door slammed shut, but I hadn't touched it. In fact, I found out later that every open door in the school slammed shut. Including Sam Tsai's, who still had his hand in his locker at the time.

"Why exactly would you want to do that?" I hissed. Igloos were warmer than my voice.

"I thought you might want to celebrate," Ryan said. His voice matched mine, ice chip for ice chip. "Do you want to go out or not? I mentioned to Sean and Samantha that we might be heading for the Black Opal tonight, and Samantha thought it might be a great way to congratulate the newest cheerleader."

"Celebrate? Cheerleader? Do you mean . . . ?"

"Didn't you know?" he grinned at me, finally catching on to my utter cluelessness. "You made the cheerleading team."

My life was becoming surreal. I looked around for the cameras but didn't see any. Yesterday, plain old Daisy Giordano. Today, Daisy Giordano, cheerleader, who was going to a trendy club with the hottest guy in school (even if it was to catch an evil-doer). I thought it seemed too good to be true—and it turned out I was absolutely right.

CHAPTER SIX

I *wondered* if Ryan still would have asked me out if I hadn't made the squad. I wanted to go out with Ryan on a real date. Badly. But this wasn't a real date. It was an investigation, a way to help my mom with the case.

I worried that Ryan, too, could have an ulterior motive for this date. Maybe I was just his camouflage and he was really trying to get closer to Samantha, so he could snake her right out from under Sean's cute but less-than-bright nose. It didn't *sound* like the Ryan I knew, but wiser men than he had done some crazy stuff in the name of love. Ryan seemed to have forgotten he ever had a crush on Samantha, but I hadn't.

Poppy and her friend Candy Thompson were hanging out in the family room when I got home. When I appeared, there was that sudden pause that happens when you enter a room where the people in it have been talking about you.

"If it isn't my little sister, the varsity cheerleader," Poppy's voice was treacle sweet.

I hadn't said anything about tryouts because I was sure I

wouldn't have a chance in Nightshade of making the squad. But I knew Poppy was probably upset that I hadn't said anything. Popularity was her thing, and cheerleading was veering into her territory.

"How did you find out so quickly?" I blurted out. "I didn't find out until Ryan told me after school just now." And Poppy didn't have a class last period, a privilege only for seniors.

"Rose is home," she answered. "She overheard the news from some kid walking home. The girl went right by the house. Whoever it was, she wasn't too happy that you made cheerleading and she didn't."

Poppy's eyes narrowed. "And Ryan told you? You two have been hanging out a lot lately." I could practically see the air quotes in the way she said "hanging out."

"We're just friends," I said. Lame, I knew, but the truth was. I didn't know what was going on with Ryan and me. If I admitted as much, Poppy would just tell me to ask him, and I couldn't think of anything more terrifying than *that*.

"Friends, huh?" Candy said. "That's not what I heard." Candy couldn't keep a secret, so she didn't even bother to try. Another reason for not wanting to talk in front of Poppy's curious friend.

That's the downside (one of many) of small-town life. Gossip was a recreational sport in Nightshade. I wondered if Samantha had been the one doing the talking. She'd certainly been the culprit back in sixth grade, which was something I'd never forgiven her for.

Poppy, for once, didn't move in for the kill. "We have more important things to talk about than my little sis's boring love life, Candy," she said, with a sniff.

Thankfully, Candy took the hint and they moved on to dissecting someone else. I made my escape upstairs. I needed to figure out what to wear. I knew Samantha would appear in something fabulous, but I had no idea what to wear to a club.

But first, I had to ask Rose something. I knocked on her bedroom door.

"Come in, Daisy," she called. "Congratulations on making the cheerleading squad," she said without even looking up from her laptop.

"Thanks," I said. I cleared my throat. "Hey, I need to ask you something."

"Shoot," she said. Rose was the smartest person I knew. Talking to her was better than a trip to the library.

"What do you know about the ankh?"

"Ancient Egyptian symbol?" Rose thought for a moment. "I'm pretty sure it represents immortality." She typed something into her computer. Gotta love that Google. "Here we go. It says here that tomb paintings often show the deities of the afterlife giving the ankh to a mummy. It's like giving them the gift of life."

My heart jumped. "So you're saying it brings dead people back to life? Like . . . vampires?"

Rose shut her laptop with a loud snap. "Vampires? Daisy, what are you getting at?"

"Nothing," I said. I was determined to solve the mystery without the benefit of my sisters' psychic powers. Still, I couldn't resist asking Rose how it was going on her end. "So, have you been able to help Mom with that case?"

Rose shook her head and sighed. "Not much," she said. "Not yet, anyway." She looked eager to change the subject. "It's getting late. I've got to go." She rose from the bed.

"Where are you off to tonight?"

"Just the library." After a quick once-over in the mirror, she pulled on a jacket and rushed past me to the stairs.

"Aren't you forgetting something?" I dangled her backpack in front of her. Rose never went to the library without it.

"Oh, yeah," she said and rushed back to grab it. "Thanks." She really *was* absentminded lately.

After Rose was gone, I went to my room to get ready. I rifled through my closet and despaired at the idea of finding anything remotely stylish. The thought briefly crossed my mind that I could borrow something from Poppy, but then I remembered the Dairy Queen incident and decided against it. I looked at the pile of clothes on my bed. There had to be at least one outfit suitable for clubbing.

I was just about to give up when a door slammed downstairs, and a few minutes later, Poppy appeared in my doorway.

"I knew it," she crowed. "You *do* have a date with a hot guy. Ryan Mendez, huh?"

"Where's Candy?" I asked.

"She left," Poppy said. "I knew you'd never spill in front of her, so I told her I had homework. Candy's allergic to homework."

I breathed a sigh of relief and said to her, "It's not exactly a date. We're going to the Black Opal to investigate."

"Interesting," Poppy said. "What are you investigating, each other?"

"Grow up, Poppy!" I snarled, "We're trying to help Mom and Chief Mendez on the case," I said.

"Is that all you are planning on doing?" she said with a mischievous glint in her eye.

"Please stop it. I'm nervous enough about this. And I have no idea what to wear."

She studied the pile on my bed with a look of concentration. "No, no, and no!" she said, and a T-shirt, a pair of capris, and a dress floated back into my closet and hung themselves back up neatly.

One by one, my clothes returned to the closet, until there was a small pile left on the bed.

Poppy snapped her fingers. "Wait a minute. I think I have a top that will match your eyes perfectly." A minute later, a silky periwinkle top floated into my room. "Here, try this on with this skirt," she said.

"I just thought of something," I said. "I can't go! I haven't made dinner." Suddenly, I was terrified at the prospect of spending time with Ryan, even though it wasn't a real date. But Poppy caught on.

"Don't worry about it," she said. "You and Ryan have been friends for ages. You'll have a great time, so stop worrying."

"Thanks, Poppy," I said. This was the side of Poppy I hadn't seen in a long time. I wasn't sure what had brought out her good side, but I was grateful something had.

"And I'll handle dinner," she added. She chuckled at my look of horror. "Don't worry, I won't touch your precious pots and pans. I'll order a pizza."

"What time is he going to pick you up?" she asked.

"He said seven." What if he didn't show?

Poppy looked at the clock. It read 5:00. "You'd better get in the shower," she said, shoving me toward the bathroom. "You don't have much time."

Not much time? It took me fifteen minutes to get ready normally, half an hour when I really worked at it. But that was before Poppy got ahold of me.

After a long shower, I found Poppy inspecting three outfits she'd deemed worthy of a first date.

"The Black Opal won't let you in unless you dress to impress," she warned.

I noticed that the denim skirt I bought last month was the only option from my own wardrobe. She'd paired it with a burgundy boho top with full sleeves and with heels that could double as an assault weapon. There was also a short deep blue dress with a plunging neckline that I vetoed immediately. I wanted Ryan to like me for more than just my looks. The third outfit included Rose's favorite jeans, the superexpensive ones that fit me perfectly, Poppy's periwinkle top, and shoes I could actually walk in. Naturally, I chose the last outfit.

Poppy nodded her approval. "Now get dressed and I'll do your hair and makeup."

As Poppy did her magic, I wondered if all the primping was worth it. "There," she said. "All done. Take a look."

I stepped in front of the full-length mirror hanging on my closet door. I was speechless. Poppy had worked a miracle. My eyes magically looked bigger and bluer than ever, my lashes were impossibly long, and my hair looked expertly tousled, not the usual flyaway mess. For the first time, I could see my own resemblance to my glamorous mother and sisters.

"It's a good thing Mom's working late again tonight," she commented. "She'd have a heart attack to see you looking like this. She still thinks you're five."

"Poppy, thanks so much!" I gave her a hug. She hugged me back, just for a second, and then said, "Oh, don't worry. I'll think of some way you can repay me."

Whatever torture she had dreamed up in repayment would totally be worth it, I thought, but I knew Poppy well enough not to say it out loud.

The doorbell rang and I looked at my watch. It was five to seven.

"He's early," Poppy said. "He's got it bad."

We started for the door, but then I thought of something. "Hey, Poppy?"

"Yeah?" She paused at the top of the stairs.

I gestured to my borrowed finery. "This isn't going to float off my back at midnight, is it?"

"Of course not," she replied. "I gave you permission to borrow this outfit. And besides, Ryan Mendez is a million times hotter than Brian Miller."

Poppy went into the kitchen while I answered the door. For a minute, I stared at Ryan and forgot to breathe. He looked amazing. His shirt matched his green eyes. We locked gazes, and neither of us would look away.

"Hi," he said, smiling softly. "Wow."

"Hi," I said, still looking into his eyes.

"Are you ready to go?" he asked. "Or maybe I should come in and say hi to your mom before we leave."

I opened the door wider to let him in. "Mom's not home from work yet. I think she's still working on that case."

Ryan shifted his feet nervously but took one step inside. "Really? Dad's still working, too," he said. "Maybe we should just go, then."

I grabbed my purse. "Poppy, we're leaving. Let Mom know where I am, okay?"

She came out of the kitchen with the cordless in her hand.

"Have fun, you guys." Then, into the phone, "That's a large pie, with everything, extra cheese, and *lots* of anchovies."

I made a face. I couldn't help it. I hated anchovies, but Poppy loved them. It was her chance to munch on the fishy morsels to her heart's content.

"You don't like anchovies, huh?" Ryan said. "I'll have to remember that for next time."

Next time, huh? There was going to be a next time. I smiled at him. This was going to be a great evening. That's what I thought, anyway. I was definitely not the psychic in the family.

CHAPTER SEVEN

The evening started to go downhill as soon as I got into Ryan's car and saw Samantha sitting in the front seat. Sean was in the backseat, and he looked about as happy as I felt, which was not at all.

Ryan opened the rear passenger door for me and shot me an apologetic look. "Samantha gets carsick in the back," he explained.

I told myself it wasn't jealousy that was making me queasy.

"I hope you don't mind," Samantha said sweetly. "Queasy stomach."

"I know the feeling," I muttered, but in a louder voice I said, "Not at all. Sean and I can talk about"—I searched frantically for something we could possibly have in common, until I realized he was in my English class—"English."

Samantha laughed. "That's kind of a sore subject," she said.

Sean looked at me, stony faced. "I'm flunking it."

"Oh," I said.

On the way to the club, Samantha and Ryan chatted easily in the front of the car, while Sean and I maintained an awkward silence in the backseat. I frowned when I noticed how often she managed to touch Ryan's arm in the course of casual conversation.

She was dressed entirely in alabaster white, from her top to her gorgeous leather boots. Who buys white leather boots? You could wear them maybe once without getting them dirty. The Devereauxs did have money to burn, but it seemed excessive, even for Samantha.

She caught me staring at her outfit and said, "White is the color of mourning in China." So she was going to dress for death in all seven continents? And designer dead, I'd wager.

The ankh around her neck gleamed in the dark, and I remembered what Rose had told me about the history of the symbol. Why was Samantha wearing a symbol of the afterlife? And why the extreme new look? She hadn't told me the truth earlier. There was more to her new look than boredom. I just hoped it didn't involve vampirism.

Ryan's eyes met mine in the rearview mirror. "Daisy, are you okay back there? You've been awfully quiet."

"I'm fine, Ryan," I said. But I wasn't. Inside, I was kicking myself for ever agreeing to this. It was obvious that Samantha planned to monopolize Ryan for the rest of the night. That's why she had been so nice to me before. Just to lure me into a false sense of security.

I wanted to make it through the night with a shred of dignity intact. I was not going to let her see that she was getting to me.

The club parking lot was crowded already, but Ryan managed to find a spot at the far end. To my surprise, he came to my door and opened it for me, before helping me out. He left Samantha to fend for herself until Sean caught a clue and rushed over to open her door.

Ryan kept my hand in his as we walked to the door of the club. There was a long line, but Samantha marched to the front and immediately started flirting with the guy at the door.

The rest of us hung back, but then I heard someone calling my name. "Daisy? Daisy Giordano, is that you?" The guy at the door was Nicholas Bone.

"Uh, hi, Nicholas," I said. What was he doing working at the Black Opal when his family had a perfectly good mortuary? And why was he being so nice? When he had dated my sister, I wasn't sure that he could tell Poppy and me apart. Or even wanted to. He had been quiet, surly even, whenever he'd been at the house to pick up Rose. Now he stood there beaming at me like we were long-lost pals.

"Are these your friends?" His brandy-colored eyes gleamed.

I could understand what Rose had seen in him. He was handsome and tall, with pale skin, reddish brown hair, and those strange eyes. His hair was the exact shade of our Irish setter, Sparky, who died of old age last year.

I nodded and Nicholas held open the velvet rope. "Go ahead."

He gestured toward the door. "I can't make an old friend wait in this line."

I glanced at the crowd and hesitated. There were a few groans here and there, but most people seemed resigned to us cutting the line. And I had a curfew. If I didn't cut in line, I might not have any time to snoop around.

Samantha grabbed my arm and propelled me forward. "You heard the man, Giordano."

Nicholas stamped our hands and I checked the mark. It matched the one the dead girl had. Then Samantha swept through the door with Sean right behind her. Ryan and I trailed behind them.

She was getting plenty of stares. She looked like a gravedigger's dream date in her strapless metallic white top and scrap of lace that passed for a skirt, fishnet thigh-high stockings and those white boots. Fortunately, she left her coffin at home tonight— too unwieldy for the dance floor. Sean was handing out dirty looks like Halloween candy. I hoped there wouldn't be a brawl.

It was early enough that there were still a few tables available. We grabbed a booth, and Samantha and I slid into the middle with Sean on her side and Ryan on mine. I was surprised that she hadn't found a way to have a guy on either side of her, but the night was still young.

Sean and Ryan talked football while Samantha looked to see if anyone was noticing her (they were) and I watched the crowd. I wondered if any of these people had been here on the same night as the dead girl. Maybe I could talk to some of them and find out.

But at the moment, I was too nervous to say anything. Ryan had dropped my hand when we sat down, but he kept one hand on my knee. It was distracting, not entirely in a bad way. I reminded myself that I was here for sleuthing, not flirting. But I didn't take his hand off my knee.

A server came by and took our order as we waited for the first band to take the stage. "What can I get you?" he asked, after introducing himself and rattling off the drinks specials. He didn't seem to notice or care that our hands were clearly marked with the underage stamp. We ordered sodas and appetizers, but our waiter didn't seem to be in much of a hurry to trot back to the kitchen to place it.

"Are you here for Side Effects May Vary?" he asked.

"What?" I said.

"The band," he said. "They're a local favorite."

Samantha said, "And I heard they just signed a major record deal."

The club started to fill up. I recognized a couple of kids from school. Samantha's best friend, Jordan, was on the dance floor with a couple of the other cheerleaders.

Penny Edwards made a beeline for us, dragging her mini-coffin behind her. Only Penny would bring something the size of a small car to a club. There was some swearing involved when the coffin thumped against random shins and feet as Penny made her way toward us.

I relaxed a little bit. Ryan wasn't hanging on Samantha's every word. In fact, it seemed like he barely noticed her at all.

I made an attempt at friendliness. "So have you ever heard Side Effects May Vary play before?" I asked.

Samantha seemed amused by the question. "Of course. We come here all the time," she said.

"You and Sean?" Somehow, the Black Opal didn't seem to be Sean's scene, despite the fact that he was one of the popular kids.

"No, Jordan, Rachel, and me mostly, but some of the other girls on the squad sometimes."

"I come here all the time, too," Penny bragged.

"I've never been here before," I said casually, hoping for more information.

"Big surprise," Penny muttered.

I ignored her. "So, have you ever seen anyone . . . strange hanging around here?" I asked. It was entirely possible that the dead girl met her killer at this very club.

Samantha looked at me like I had two heads. "Strange? Take a look around, Giordano," she snapped.

She had a point. The room was filled with some unusual people, even by Nightshade standards. There was a guy wearing a clown costume, a woman who glowed like her skin had been covered in phosphorus, and a beautiful girl in a fire engine red cowboy hat, a bikini top, and shorts. None of them looked like killers, but you never know.

But before our semicourteous conversation could deteriorate any further, a tall man wearing a baggy checked suit and creepers on his feet strode to the microphone. "Please give it up for Side Effects May Vary!" he said.

The audience went wild, whistling and cheering.

The band took the stage and started things off with a rousing cover of the Ramones' "Rock 'n' Roll High School." The lead singer had a raspy, sexy voice, but the bass guitarist was truly eye-catching. She wore a naughty nurse's uniform paired with leopard-print tights, six-inch white plastic heels, and a towering hot pink hairdo that was obviously a wig. Her makeup looked like she had applied it with a trowel, but even with gunk on her face, there was something about her that seemed familiar.

"Let's go!" Samantha said, cutting off Penny midgrovel. "Penny, stay here and guard our table. We're going to dance." She grabbed Sean's hand and dragged him out of the booth. Then she turned and put a hand on her hip. "Daisy, are you coming?"

I looked at Ryan and raised one eyebrow in question. He took my hand and we followed Sean and Samantha to the dance floor. I felt sorry for Penny, but she seemed perfectly thrilled to be allowed to play watchdog for Samantha.

Ryan was a great dancer. A lot of guys weren't, at least in my limited experience. Take Sean, for instance. He danced like he was running for a touchdown. Zig, zag, shoulder tucked in. He'd make a motion like he was throwing a long pass and then start the sequence over again.

Samantha, on the other hand, had natural rhythm and some slick moves. She looked pretty lively for a girl obsessed with death.

We danced until the band took a break. I watched the bassist as she walked offstage. There was definitely something familiar about her. It nagged at me, but as we went back to the table, I saw a face that was even more familiar.

Rose was at the Black Opal! Definitely unlike my studious sister. She didn't see me, but made a beeline for Nicholas in the corner. It was safe to say Rose knew her ex was in town. By the way she was kissing him, I wasn't too sure he *was* her ex.

She had told me earlier that she was going to the library, yet here she was, practically devouring the mortician's son. Public displays of affection weren't like Rose at all. "I'm going to the bathroom," I said.

"Daisy," Ryan said, "maybe I should go with . . ." He trailed off when he saw my look of mortification. "Just be careful, okay?"

"I will," I said. But as I headed for Rose and Nicholas, they left their table and disappeared down the hallway I assumed led to the bathroom. I took off after them, but working my way through the crowd slowed me down.

By the time I made it to the hallway, there was no sign of them. A couple was pressed against each other in the corner by the pay phone, but it wasn't Nicholas and Rose. A distinct chemical odor wafted down the hall. It smelled like Aqua Net and cigarettes. I stood by the bathroom door, deciding what to do next. That's when I heard the scream. It sounded like it was coming from the women's restroom.

I ran into the bathroom. As I entered, I passed someone going the other way and caught a glimpse of white as she ran by me.

At first I thought the bathroom was empty, and badly in need of some cleaning. The aerosol odor was stronger in there, but mingling with that odor was another smell: sweat and stale perfume.

I turned to leave, but caught a glimpse of a cowboy hat lying on the floor in one of the bathroom stalls. And that's when I found the body.

CHAPTER EIGHT

I froze, unable to move for a moment. Please, don't let it be Rose, my mind repeated over and over as I drew closer to the crumpled figure lying on the floor of the bathroom stall. I opened the stall door slowly, reluctant to see. I could tell right away that it wasn't my sister, and I could breathe again.

I stooped down and gingerly checked for a pulse. Her wrist was so cold that I thought for sure she was already dead. Just when I was ready to give up, I felt a weak beat.

Then I heard, ever so faintly, *Help me. Please help me,* but the sound was in my head, not in my ears. Then nothing. Whatever or whoever I had heard had stopped the transmission. Either I was losing my mind or there was something seriously spooky going on here. I stared at the girl, but she was still unconscious.

I ran outside and prayed that the couple by the pay phone would still be there. They were. "Get help!" I yelled. "There's an unconscious girl in the bathroom." They jumped apart and stared at me. "Go!" I shouted.

"I'm a paramedic," the guy said. "Off duty," he added, in case I thought he was slacking on the job. "Show me where she is. Vanessa, you call an ambulance." Vanessa nodded and rummaged for her cell phone. Paramedic guy and I raced back to the bathroom and he immediately started CPR. God, why hadn't I learned CPR? I stood there, feeling completely helpless.

It seemed like it took hours, but I finally heard the sound of the sirens coming near.

Down the hall the lights were up, and club-goers were milling around, trying to get a glimpse of the excitement.

I waited until the paramedics had steered the gurney through the bathroom door, then I headed back to our table. Samantha rushed up to me. "Daisy, where have you been? We heard a girl had been murdered. Ryan was going crazy, but I told him you were probably fine."

"I was a little tied up," I said.

"If you didn't want to go out with him, you should have just said no," she said. "You didn't have to avoid him all night."

"I wasn't avoiding him," I said, "and besides, this wasn't a real date."

Samantha looked unconvinced. So did Ryan, who appeared at that minute. I wondered if he heard the last part of our conversation. It was hard to tell. His face was expressionless, but he looked like he was holding something in check.

Explanation time. "I found the girl everyone is talking about,"

I blurted out to him. "When I went to the bathroom. But she wasn't murdered. She was still alive when I found her, just unconscious."

His expression softened a little. "Are you okay?"

"I'm fine," I assured him. He put an arm around me and gave me a hug, which I took as an encouraging sign. "Daisy," he said into my ear, "I was so worried."

"I didn't mean to worry you," I said, "but I had to get help, and then I couldn't just leave her there alone." I shuddered. "It was awful, Ryan."

"Why don't we take off?" he suggested. "I don't think any-body's in the mood to stay anyway."

Samantha and Sean had drifted over to a cluster of kids from school, so we went over to round them up.

"Let's get going," Ryan said. "Daisy's had a rough night."

"Daisy found that girl," Samantha told Penny Edwards. It'd be all over school tomorrow.

"Really?" Penny said eagerly. "What was it like?"

"I don't really want to talk about it," I said. "I just want to go home."

Surprisingly, Samantha didn't argue. As we left the club, though, Ryan's dad pulled up in a squad car. Just great.

I looked over at Ryan and he gave my hand a comforting squeeze. My mother wouldn't be happy when Chief Mendez told her what happened at the club.

Chief Mendez said, "It came over the scanner about an

incident at the Black Opal and I remembered you were taking your date here tonight. You kids okay?"

"We're fine," Ryan said, "but Daisy found her. She's a little shaken up, so I'm taking her home."

"She's still alive," I offered, "or at least she was when the ambulance got here." I shuddered as I remembered the faint voice calling for help. A voice only in my head, I reminded myself.

The chief looked troubled. "Daisy, I want you and your friends to be careful," he said. "It's beginning to seem like someone is preying on young girls around here."

"I'm always careful," I said. I didn't mention that I was also determined to catch the culprit before someone else ended up dead.

Chief Mendez asked me a few questions, and I answered them as best I could. I didn't tell him about the weird feeling I'd had—like I'd been in someone else's head.

"Thank you, Daisy," he said. "I'll call you if I have anything else. But we'll probably learn more when we talk to the victim. Ryan, make sure you get her home safe."

We said good-bye to Ryan's dad and walked back to the car. Ryan opened the car door—the front passenger door this time— and helped me inside. Samantha fumed at the curb for a second and then stomped to the back door, tapping her foot until Sean finally opened it for her.

No one spoke on the ride home. We got to Samantha's house first. "Daisy, meet me in the gym at 7:00 A.M. sharp," she instructed, before getting out of the car. "There's a pep rally tomorrow afternoon and I have to go over the routine with you." With that, she flounced up the sidewalk toward her dark house.

Sean got out of the car, too, and came around to the driver's side window.

"See ya later," he said. "I'm going to walk Samantha to the door."

Ryan played it cool, but I saw a tinge of red creep into his cheeks. He put the car in gear and we continued home. I hadn't had time to think about it before, but this was the first time Ryan and I had been alone all night.

Despite the fact that it had been the least romantic first date in the history of first dates, I still wanted Ryan to kiss me.

He seemed to be taking his time about it, though. I draped my arm casually over the seat, so close that I could almost touch the curls that caressed the nape of his neck. He kept his attention on the road. I was glad he was a safe driver and all, but there were plenty of scenic views, aka romantic spots to park.

Then again, I'd seen enough horror movies to know that making out in a secluded spot was just inviting trouble, especially when there was someone or something out there attacking teenage girls. Going home like Chief Mendez had ordered suddenly held tremendous appeal.

But then I saw something on the road in front of us that changed my mind. A silver gray luxury car.

"Ryan!" I shrieked. "Follow that car! I think Rose is in it."

"Rose?" Ryan asked. "But isn't that Nicholas Bone's car?"

Naturally, he would remember the car that had almost run him over. I hadn't told Ryan about seeing Rose and Nicholas together at the club or their conspicuous absence following the attack, either.

It wasn't hard to trail them, because there weren't too many cars on the road at that time of night and the full moon gave us plenty of illumination, but Ryan kept way back so they wouldn't notice us following them.

"What is she doing?" I said crossly. Why was Rose getting involved with Nicholas again? It took her more than a year to get over him last time.

The car pulled into the alleyway behind Mort's Mortuary and stopped.

"I'll park around the corner," Ryan said, "preferably on a nice deserted side street. There's no sense in advertising our presence."

He took my hand as we walked, but I was too worried about Rose to enjoy it very much. As we drew closer to the back entrance of the mortuary, another car door slammed.

I counted twelve other cars; thirteen, including the one Rose had arrived in. Thirteen, a mortician's dozen.

Something was definitely up at Mort's tonight. I wouldn't put it past Nicholas to have a party in his father's place of business, but it wasn't like Rose to attend something like that. Although love does make people do crazy stuff. Or in my sister's case, stupid stuff like dating Nicholas in the first place. I still couldn't believe he dumped her without a word, just stopped calling and started avoiding.

Ryan waited a few minutes and then tried the back door. It creaked open with an absurdly loud noise.

We could hear the low murmur of voices coming from somewhere at the front of the building. This was it.

We tip-toed down the hall until we ended up in one of the smaller viewing rooms. The smell of flowers was strong. I hoped we weren't crashing some strange late-night wake.

The door was open and I went through as quietly as I could. Ryan followed behind me, but I don't think he was happy about it. We ducked into a small alcove and hoped they wouldn't see us.

The room was in shadow, lit only by the candlelight from a couple of candelabra set up near a makeshift altar of some kind. Definitely not a wake.

Rose was surrounded by creatures of the night. I couldn't believe that what I was seeing was real, but it was. I turned to Ryan and saw the same dawning realization on his face. Adrenaline pumped through my body. If creatures like this walked among us, anything was possible.

I counted four werewolves, at least six vampires, and a couple of banshees. The only person I recognized was Mrs. Mason, the president of my mom's garden club. I couldn't figure out what she was doing there, dressed in her orthopedic shoes and jogging suit, until I saw her wand. Mom had always wondered how Mrs. Mason managed to grow roses the size of a bread plate every year.

A tall hooded figure at the front of the altar said, "The Nightshade City Council meeting will now come to order." He lifted a bony hand and pulled his hood back. Instead of a face, an ivory skull gleamed in the candlelight.

City council? That was definitely not our mayor. At least I hoped it wasn't. It was hard to tell, since the guy was literally skin and bones, minus the skin.

"We have a serious problem on our hands," he continued. "As many of you already know, a body has disappeared from the morgue. A number of recent attacks in the area suggest that we're dealing with a vampire."

There was a rumble of voices as everyone began to talk at once. Skull banged on a gavel until there was silence.

"Hey!" shouted a short female vampire wearing too much lipstick (at least I hoped it was lipstick) and too little clothing. "We have nothing to do with this."

A tall undead male dressed in tight black satin pants and a frilly white shirt nodded in agreement. "We've been living in seclusion and following the rules the council set up for our kind for years. We are not responsible for these attacks."

A banshee said, in a voice like nails across a blackboard, "They didn't find fang marks on any of the bodies, so why do you think it's a vampire attacking these kids? There are many other species who feed upon the young."

Back in the alcove, pressed up against Ryan and trying not to breathe too loudly, I was wondering the same thing. I had personally seen the necks of both the girl at the morgue and the girl at the club. No bite marks on either one of them.

"The culprit is a different kind of vampire," the calorie-challenged leader boomed, "a psionic vampire. Instead of blood, this type of vampire drains its victims of their energy, their life force."

The group of blood suckers seemed to breathe a collective sigh of relief that they wouldn't be getting stakes through their hearts tonight. Although when I thought about it, did vampires have breath enough to sigh?

"So this vampire," said a doubting voice in the crowd, "it sucks souls? How does it do it?"

"Psionic vampires are rare, but very powerful," explained Skull. "The vampire hypnotizes its victim before sucking out the soul. The vamp can also create fledglings by sharing its essence, much in the same way that a blood vampire would create a fledgling by sharing its blood. Or it could be gradually feeding from several victims who don't remember a thing. The victims' energy gets lower and lower until, one day, they end up like that girl in the morgue."

I shivered and huddled closer to Ryan.

"The demon must be destroyed," said a werewolf in the crowd.

Mrs. Mason said, "If we kill the head vampire, any fledglings will become human again. But if we don't, we'll have a whole renegade colony."

Skull nodded. "We think the girl who disappeared from the morgue is the vampire's fledgling. If we can find her, she'll lead us to the vampire. We'll take a vote on it," Skull intoned. "All those for extinction of the psionic vampire, say aye."

The room rang with affirmatives, but the cluster of vampires protested loudly.

Skull banged on his gavel. When the room grew silent, he said, "Those opposed, please say nay."

"Nay," shouted the vampires. "We do not condone the wanton destruction of one of our kind," the tall male vampire said.

"I must remind you that all paranormal creatures have agreed to abide by the decisions of this council," Skull said. "Do you formally challenge this authority?"

The woman vamp, who I privately nicknamed Scarlet because of her bright red lips, moved forward to speak, but the tall male put a hand on her arm. "We withdraw our objections at this time," he said, bowing low, before gesturing to the other vampires. They exited, with the leader's hand still tight on Scarlet's arm.

"Motion passed," Skull pronounced. "Any new business?"

A russet-colored werewolf stepped forward. "New-member business." The voice coming from the creature belonged to Nicholas Bone. My sister was dating a werewolf.

Skull picked up a long, ornate dagger and motioned Rose to

the front of the room. He took her by the wrist. There would be no ceremonies that included daggers and Giordanos tonight, not if I could stop it. I made a motion forward, but Ryan held me back. I smothered a scream, but I wasn't quick enough.

Rose looked around like she was searching for someone. *Daisy, you are in so much trouble,* her voice said in my mind. *I'm fine. But you won't be if you don't leave. Now.*

I ducked my head back into the alcove and prayed no one else had spotted us.

Skull dropped the dagger and swore.

A werewolf with a beautiful silver coat froze and sniffed the air.

I heard a low growl. A shiver went down my spine. We were in trouble. There was what sounded like a very pissed-off puppy right beside us.

"Ryan?" I said softly.

"Yes?" he said, his eyes searching the shadows.

"I think it's time to leave," I said.

"Daisy," he replied, "it's time to run."

He grabbed my hand and we bolted. I was too busy running for my life to worry about whether or not anyone was following us.

Then, I heard a loud panting behind us. I sped up, cursing all those nights I'd stayed home with a pint of Ben & Jerry's instead of heading to the gym.

We ran the block it took to get to Ryan's car. He slammed it into gear and we took off.

"Maybe I should join the track team," I joked weakly.

When we got to our house, Mom's car was in the driveway, but there wasn't a light on in her room. She must have already gone to bed.

I made some hot chocolate, and Ryan and I sat in the living room waiting for Rose to come home. Finally, she burst in the front door, thankfully unscathed, but clearly angry. "Daisy, what were you doing there?"

"Following you," I said. Rose stared at me with a strange expression on her face.

"What?" I whispered to Ryan.

"You were talking like Rose had asked you a question," he said.

"She did," I said. Now I was the confused one.

"No, she didn't, Daisy," he said. "She just had a really annoyed look on her face, which means . . ."

"Which means what?"

"That you read her mind," he said.

"But I can't read minds." My mind tried to process the information, but I had more immediate concerns; namely, one ticked-off big sis.

Rose stood in front of me with her hands on her hips. "Do you know how long it took me to convince Nicholas to let me be initiated? And then you barge in and ruin it."

"Ruin *what* exactly?"

"A secret-society meeting," she said.

"Not very secret," I commented. She glared at me, but I continued anyway. "I mean, it's not like Mort's Mortuary is the Batcave or anything. It's only a block off Main Street."

Poppy must have heard us, because she wandered in and plopped down in the big leather chair. "How'd it go?" she asked Rose.

"Not well," she said. "There was a . . . complication."

"Do you mean that your boyfriend is in a secret society that evidently makes decisions about paranormal matters, or the part where he's a werewolf?"

Whatever Rose had been doing, it was obvious that Poppy knew about it. My sisters, as usual, were keeping secrets from me.

"Daisy, don't look like that," Poppy said. "Rose only told me tonight because she needed to let someone know where she was, just in case."

"But you knew that Nicholas was of the furry persuasion?" I asked.

"That's why he broke up with her before," Poppy admitted. "He'd just found out about being a werewolf."

"But neither of you said a word to me," I said. Left out as usual.

"I was going to, honestly, Daisy, but Nicholas asked me not to say anything."

"Go on," I said.

Rose sighed. "You can't say anything to anybody about this," she said. "You know I've been helping Mom with this case. And you know that I've been . . . talking to Nicholas again. He told me there's a secret society in Nightshade that might be able to help."

"And Nicholas Bone is a member?"

"One of them," she admitted. Her glance strayed to Ryan's face with a particular intensity. What was going on? "The thirteen original families who settled Nightshade started it ages ago."

"The original thirteen?" Ryan said. "You're sure?"

Rose nodded, studying him closely. I stared at her and then glanced at Ryan. He seemed shocked by what he'd heard. "I— I've got to go. Curfew." He stood and walked out the door without a good-bye.

"What's with him?" I wondered, staring at the empty doorway. But my mind was still reeling. I quickly turned my attention back to Rose. "So, this secret society. What do they do? Are they good or bad?" The questions tumbled out of my mouth.

"I don't know," she said. "Nicholas wouldn't tell me much, but I do know they make judgments about the . . . less than normal occurrences in Nightshade."

"You mean the supernatural stuff? You think they're the good guys? That dagger didn't exactly make me think of white knights and chivalry," I said.

"Nicholas would never do anything to hurt me," she said stubbornly.

I wasn't so sure, but I supposed I'd be snippy, too, if my boyfriend was an overgrown furball. There was a lot of stuff for me to digest: a soul-sucking vampire on the loose, my sister's boyfriend being a werewolf, and a secret society, which meant that the town's founding fathers (and mothers) probably weren't human. Nightshade was even weirder than I had thought.

CHAPTER NINE

As worn out as I was from the events of the previous night, on Friday morning my cheerleading career was off to a flying start. Samantha met me and the other new cheerleaders in the gym to give us our uniforms and teach us some of the routines. I had a hard time getting used to walking down the halls of Nightshade High in my cheerleading uniform. I tugged down the short skirt when I saw Wyatt Pearson staring at my legs.

When I saw Ryan and waved at him, my sweater rode up and bared a sliver of midriff skin. I felt exposed and slightly ridiculous. Ryan's smile of appreciation did make me feel better, though. So did the way he put his arm around me as he walked me to class.

"I'm not ready for this," I said.

"For class?" Ryan said.

"For the pep rally," I said. "I can't cheer in front of the whole school."

He brushed a stray lock of hair away from my face. "You'll be great," he said. "But I'm not sure I like the way all the guys are checking you out."

"Nobody even knew my name before now," I scoffed. "It's just the uniform."

"No," he said softly. "It's you. And I knew your name."

I smiled at him. "I know."

The bell rang, and Ryan sprinted to his class. I watched him go before I went into mine.

The only good thing about the pep rally was that I got out of class early. I met the other girls in the gym after sixth period. Miss Foster wasn't there yet.

Everyone was gathered around Samantha. She frowned when she saw me. "You're late, Daisy."

"I had a test," I explained.

She handed me a small, brightly wrapped box. I noticed that the other cheerleaders were holding similar packages.

"What's this?"

She smiled at me. "Just a little something. Open it!"

I looked at her warily. She didn't look like a vampire, despite her pale skin, black wardrobe, and bloodred lips. She looked like someone I could trust. Too bad I didn't believe it, not for a second. I didn't know whether or not she was the vamp, but I did know that Samantha Devereaux wasn't ever nice, not without a reason.

The other girls tore through the wrappings. I opened mine slowly and found a beautiful silver bracelet. Dangling from it was a small black symbol.

"It's an ankh," Jordan said. She was right. It was the same symbol as the one on Samantha's pendant.

The girls clustered around Samantha. "I love it," Penny cooed.

I stood there, lost in thought as the squad thanked Samantha. Why was she suddenly handing out presents? And why an ankh?

Samantha looked at me expectantly. I focused and realized she was waiting for a thank-you.

"Thanks," I said. "It's lovely."

"Well, put it on," she said. "We don't have much time. I want everyone to wear them to the pep rally."

I had intended to slip it into my pocket, but our uniforms didn't have pockets. Samantha took it from me and fastened it on my wrist.

She stepped back and surveyed me for a long moment. "That's better," she said.

Miss Foster arrived as we were warming up. She was dressed in bright white designer sweats with red trim. "Let's get ready, girls. In formation." She blew her whistle.

Samantha said, "Good luck, Daisy!" Before I could respond, she added. "And don't forget, you're a base during the pyramid formation."

I was surprised she didn't make a snide remark about my weight. There were two categories of cheerleaders, flyers and bases. The flyers were the tiniest of the tiny and the bases, well, weren't. I was going to be on the bottom of the pyramid. I just had to smile while I supported the entire squad on my back.

And speaking of getting to the bottom of things, I had some sleuthing to do. I wanted to find out what the jewelry meant. After finding out from Rose that the ankh was associated with resurrection and the afterlife, I had a hunch I wasn't going to like the answer.

I didn't like wearing it, but there was no way I could take it off now, standing in front of the whole school.

We stood in formation while Principal Amador droned on. I thought my leg was going to cramp and bent down to rub it. Samantha frowned at me and shook her head. I quickly straightened.

Ryan and the rest of the football players sat in the first row. Great—he'd have a perfect view if I made a complete fool of myself.

The music started, and that was our cue. I hoped I would remember the routine. Thankfully, Samantha put me near the back, so no one noticed when I stumbled. No such luck. Penny smirked at me. A few minutes later, she nearly crushed my hand when she stepped on it climbing on my back for the pyramid.

As soon as the pyramid had formed, a figure dressed in a short black skirt and top darted in front of us. I saw a flash of red hair. Peering out of the corner of my eye, I was stunned to see that it was the missing dead girl.

I made an involuntary movement and Samantha, in the row above me, said through gritted teeth, "Daisy, don't you dare move. If you do, we'll all come tumbling down on top of you."

She didn't say "you idiot," but she didn't need to. It was still a struggle to remain still as a statue while the figure whirled and twirled and finally went into an impossibly long set of cartwheels and wheeled herself right out of the gym.

The room rang with applause.

I searched the stands for Ryan. He looked confused by my shocked expression, but he didn't recognize the show-off as the dead girl—only I had seen her in the morgue.

I wished I could run after her, but there was nothing I could do but watch her slip away. I caught Poppy's eye and she mouthed, "What's wrong?" from her seat in the stands.

It was too late. I just shook my head. She gave me a big thumbs-up, probably thinking I was just nervous about my performance.

Dedicated dieters or not, I felt like my back was going to break under the weight of the other cheerleaders. Finally, we got out of the pyramid formation.

Mr. Amador said, "Please give a round of applause for Coach

Rainer Wullf and the Nightshade Sea Monsters varsity football team!"

I stood in a straight line with the other cheerleaders and shouted to get the crowd fired up, but my mind wasn't on "Go, Fight, Win"—it was on the dead girl's appearance at my school.

After the rally, the cheerleaders decided to change and grab something to eat. It wouldn't do to get anything on the uniforms, not before a game.

Sam and I were the only ones left in the locker room changing into street clothes when Mrs. Devereaux swept into the room in a cloud of Chanel.

What was she doing here? Mrs. Devereaux was usually too busy trying to make the San Francisco society pages to pay any attention to her own daughter. Or at least that's what my mom, who rarely said anything negative about anyone, had told me.

But there Mrs. Devereaux was in all her couture glory.

"Samantha," she said, kissing the air a few inches from Samantha's face.

"Mother, you made it to the pep rally!" Sam's face lit up.

"No, dear, I was in town for a meeting with our bankers," Mrs. Devereaux said.

Samantha's smile disappeared.

"What is that atrocity you're wearing?" Mrs. Devereaux said, after looking Samantha over. "You look absolutely ghastly."

Ghastly? Sam had changed into a flowing dress in gray. It looked like someone had draped a huge spiderweb over her, but it wasn't the strangest outfit I'd seen her in lately. And Sam still looked gorgeous.

I was surprised to see a look of satisfaction on Samantha's face. Could it be that she was adopting the ghoul look just to irritate her mother?

"You don't like it?" Samantha asked, hiding a smile.

"Heavens no," Mrs. Devereaux replied. "The next time I'm in town, I must take you shopping for something decent."

"Next time?" Samantha said. "You're leaving already?"

"I'm afraid I must," her mother replied. "I have a fund-raiser to attend this evening."

The smile left Samantha's face for a second, before she plastered it back on. "It's okay," she said airily. "I have lots to do, too, but I did need to ask you just one thing. Daisy, if you'll excuse us?"

They walked to one end of the locker room and stood there talking for a few minutes. I couldn't hear what they were saying, but I could tell from their body language that Samantha was asking for something and her mother was saying no.

After their low-voiced conversation, Mrs. Devereaux turned and left, not even bothering to hug Sam good-bye or tell her when she'd see her again.

As nasty as Sam could be, it was impossible not to feel bad for her at that moment, as she stared at the door her mom disappeared through.

After a few seconds, she turned to me. "Daisy, quit staring," she snapped. "Don't you have anything better to do?"

I shrugged and gave her a sympathetic look, but she turned up her nose. Sam was trying to hide the hurt, but I could see it. The girl was full of secrets and I'd get them out of her eventually.

That's what friends were for, right? To be there when you needed them? Whether Samantha Devereaux and I could be considered friends was debatable, but I had a feeling that she needed me, even if she wasn't ready to admit it or to tell me what was going on.

Sam cleared her throat noisily and then changed the subject. "Can you believe that show-off Chelsea Morris?"

"No, not really," I answered her, but my mind was whirling. Besides rejoicing in the fact that I'd made it through my first pep rally without throwing up, and worrying about Sam, I also wondered where the red-haired girl had gone. Had she been a figment of my imagination?

"I bet she's trying to steal our routine. When we were in cheer camp . . ." Sam continued her story, but I had tuned her out. She thought her life was something out of *Bring It On*, but I had bigger things to worry about. Like finding the dead girl who was walking around Nightshade.

"I can't believe she had the nerve to show up at our pep rally," she said.

"What did you say?" I asked, suddenly homing in on what she was saying. "You know that girl?"

She put her hands on her hips. "That's who I've been talking about for the last five minutes. Honestly. Yes, Chelsea Morris. From cheer camp. Goes to San Carlos High. Haven't you been listening at all?"

"What else do you know about her?"

This time, I listened while Sam filled me in on everything she knew about a dead girl.

CHAPTER TEN

The football game against Quail Hollow followed the pep rally. After the game, Ryan went off with the rest of the guys to celebrate. With all the excitement, I hadn't had any time alone with Ryan to tell him what I had found out about the identity of the dead girl, and the weekend ended without a call from him. Samantha seemed to think Ryan and I were locked down as a couple, but I had my doubts.

After my last class on Monday, I hurried to my locker to meet up with Ryan for a few minutes.

I wanted to catch him before the squad showed up to drag me off to the hospital. Not that I didn't want to visit Rachel. I did, but I didn't want to go with the whole squad, like I was some sort of creature who could travel only in a pack.

Visiting Rachel was a kind, considerate thing to do. So how was it that Samantha was the one who thought of it? She didn't have a kind bone in her body. Did she? Or maybe she was just visiting to make a withdrawal, like a selfish, soul-sucking fiend. Now *that* sounded more like the Samantha I knew.

I was going up the stairs, headed for my locker, when someone grabbed me and pulled me into the shadowy stairwell. I was not in the mood to become some vamp's dinner, so I put an elbow in the ribs of the person holding me.

"Daisy, it's me," Ryan said.

"You nearly scared the life out of me," I said. "You can't go creeping around, not when there's a vampire loose."

"Sorry, I didn't think," he said. It was darker in the stairwell and much more private. Or it would have been, except it was also already occupied by two freshmen.

"Beat it!" I said, and they scampered.

"Want to come over after school?" Ryan pressed a kiss along the base of my neck and I shivered.

"I can't make it today," I told him. "Samantha asked the squad to visit Rachel in the hospital." And maybe I could poke around and find out something about Rachel's mysterious illness. If Samantha was sucking her soul, I wanted to put a stop to it.

"Sure," he said. "But I have tons of homework and I could use a little help with statistics."

"That's why you asked me to your house after school? You wanted help with your homework?" Ryan was a straight-A student.

He didn't say anything, and finally the light dawned.

"Ryan Mendez, you were trying to lure me to your house under false pretenses," I said.

"I just wanted to spend some time with you," he said. "Our first date was memorable, but we didn't get any time alone."

Date? I thought. The Black Opal fiasco was a real date? Obviously, it wasn't a very good one. Of course, an awful first date with Ryan was ten times better than a smooth date with anyone else.

"Drag," I said. "Samantha will have a conniption if I don't go to the hospital. And I'd really like to see Rachel."

"It's okay. There will be other nights."

I said, "There will, I promise."

"Is that the only reason you dragged me into the stairwell?" Ryan asked, moving closer and putting his hands around my waist.

I gave him a light punch on the arm. "*You* dragged me here, remember?"

"And now I remember why," he said softly before he kissed me.

A long moment later, I finally started to breathe again. "Ryan," I said, "Samantha is probably looking for me."

"So?" he said. He brushed a lock of hair back from my face.

"So she might see us," I said, panicking.

"She already knows we're going out," he said calmly. He cupped the back of my head to pull me in for another kiss.

"But you like her," I said.

"Of course I like her," he said. "She's Sean's girlfriend and Sean's my friend."

"No, you *like* her like her," I said. "You've had a huge crush on her since the second grade, you can't deny it."

"Daisy, that was years ago," he replied. "I also ate paste and wanted to be a fireman. I don't like Samantha Devereaux except as a friend."

"You don't?"

He kissed the side of my neck. "I. Like. You." Each word was punctuated by soft kisses. "Now please kiss me," he said.

Since he asked so nicely, I did. He did that nicely as well.

Several minutes later, I pulled myself out of his arms. "Ryan, I've got to go. The squad will be waiting."

I sprinted down the hall and then up the stairs to the main entrance. I grinned the whole way. Ryan liked me, not Samantha, not whoever else he'd been kissing in the morgue. He liked plain old Daisy Giordano.

I met Samantha and the rest of the squad coming downstairs as I was coming up. The smile disappeared from my face.

"Daisy, we've been looking everywhere for you," she snapped. "Did you forget about Rachel already?"

"No," I huffed, trying to catch my breath. "Weren't we going to meet in the parking lot?"

Samantha gave me a dead-eye stare but didn't say anything. I had a guilty feeling she knew what I'd been doing. A feeling that was confirmed when she handed me a tissue and whispered, "Your lipstick is smeared."

"Thanks." She was being nice to me and covering my

butt besides. In Samantha's case, being dead was a definite improvement.

"Let's go!" she said. "Daisy, you can ride with me. I'll show you how to put on lipstick properly. We can't have our newest cheerleader looking like a bag lady."

Okay, maybe not *that* big of an improvement.

Samantha somehow managed to get me in her car alone. I knew it might not be the smartest thing to do—spend time alone with a possible vamp—but I didn't have many friends. And she had seemed genuinely surprised when Chelsea showed up at the pep rally. Samantha wasn't *that* good an actress. She certainly wasn't fooling me with her sudden friendliness. She was going to grill me about Ryan, I just knew it.

But she didn't.

"That was fun the other night," she said. "The hanging out together part, not the finding the unconscious girl part."

"It was fun," I said. Except for the part where she sat in the front and hogged Ryan.

"We should do it again sometime," she suggested.

Samantha and I had been best friends in sixth grade. At the time, I had trusted her more than anyone, even my sisters. I didn't trust her now.

"Why are you suddenly interested in being friends, Sam?" The nickname just slipped out. I hadn't called her that for a long time.

"Daisy, I know you're still mad at me about what happened,

but it was a long time ago. People can change. I just want you to give me a chance."

She had her chance, I thought, but aloud I said, "We're on the same squad now. I can't promise that we'll ever be best friends, but I'll try to get along." And being on the squad would mean that I could keep a close eye on the dead Devereaux.

She seemed satisfied with my answer, and the talk turned to the upcoming homecoming dance.

The other girls were waiting for us in the hospital parking lot, holding a huge GET WELL SOON banner. Samantha's best friend, Jordan, had a distinct pout on her black-lipsticked face. She was probably sulking because Samantha hadn't let her ride in the car with us.

I trailed behind the group. I needed to do some digging and couldn't do it in a cluster of cheer. When we reached the elevators, I spotted a gift shop.

"I'm just going to buy Rachel some flowers," I said brightly. "I'll catch up with you upstairs. What's her room number?"

"Room 301," Samantha said. "Don't take too long."

I gave her an exasperated look. "We can't all visit her at the same time anyway. Hospital rules."

Actually, I had no idea if those were the rules, but I needed her off my back for a few minutes. What I was about to do was definitely against hospital rules, and I didn't need any witnesses.

Rose had undergone an appendectomy at this hospital last year. Not that big of a coincidence, since it was the only hospital in town, but I did learn my way around the place while she was there.

I ducked into the gift shop and grabbed a nice bouquet. Rachel was a good person and didn't deserve the weirdness that was happening to her. If Samantha was the reason for it, she was going to be sorry.

I slipped out of the elevator on the third floor just in time to see a nurse shushing my squad as they turned the corner. The nurses' station was temporarily deserted.

In the station were rows of cubbyholes. I knew from Rose's time there that the patients' charts were kept there.

I hunkered down and hoped I wouldn't be spotted. The charts were labeled only with room numbers, so I scanned the rows of files quickly, searching for 301. It wasn't there.

I stood, took a quick look around the corridor. Still no sign of any nurses. I went back to the nurses' station and surveyed the files on the desk. There it was!

I heard footsteps just as I spotted Rachel's file. I couldn't get to it in time.

I had only a few seconds to whip around to the other side. "May I help you?" A woman's voice said pleasantly.

"I'm looking for Rachel King?" I said, trying to sound innocent.

"She's in room 301. Are you one of her cheerleader friends?" The woman asked.

I nodded.

"It is visiting hours, but I'm afraid you'll have to wait until someone leaves. I'm stretching the rules as it is by allowing so many visitors at once."

"Is it all right if I wait here?"

"Certainly," she said. "There are a few chairs and some magazines right over there." She pointed to a tiny waiting area and I sat. I grabbed a magazine and thumbed through it while I tried to figure out my next move. For the next several minutes, I watched as people passed by—orderlies transporting patients, visitors, and even a doctor or two.

A bell went off somewhere and the nurse hurried down a corridor, but I couldn't make a move because the hallway was still clogged with people. A few minutes later, the traffic died down and the hallway was deserted. I kept an eye out for the desk nurse and casually ambled in the direction of the nurses' station. I reached over and grabbed Rachel's file, stuffed it under my shirt, and took off. My heart was pounding so hard it sounded like someone chasing me.

I went into the bathroom and locked the door. Until I exhaled deeply, I hadn't realized I'd been holding my breath.

I flipped through Rachel's chart and realized that I had no idea what I was reading. I didn't speak medical. I grabbed some paper towels from the dispenser and dug in my purse for something to write with. I scribbled down several words that seemed important and shoved the paper into my purse.

I took another deep breath and stuck the file back under my shirt. I grabbed my purse and left the bathroom.

From across the waiting room, I could see that the nurses' station was empty. I eased the folder from under my shirt and was about to put it back in its rightful place when I heard my name being spoken. Panic flooded my body. Busted. The folder whizzed across the room and landed on the desk.

I turned and saw Poppy.

My shoulders slumped with relief. "Poppy, thanks so much!"

"Thanks for what?"

I didn't know why she was being so modest. She'd just saved my butt by using her telekinesis. I dropped it, assuming that she just didn't want to talk about her powers in public or something, even though she'd never shown a sign of false modesty before now.

We both turned as we heard footsteps approaching.

"Don't say anything," I whispered. "I'll explain later."

It was the same nurse from before. "Some of the girls have left," she said. "So you can go visit your friend now."

I grabbed the flowers, and Poppy and I headed to Rachel's room.

"What are you doing here?" I asked her.

"Same as you," she said. "Visiting Rachel." It made sense. Rachel and Poppy both hung with the popular people, but I wasn't convinced. I raised an eyebrow.

"Okay," Poppy said in a whisper, "I was snooping, obviously, just like you were."

Rachel had a private room, which was decorated in peach

and white. The spicy smell of the roses and lilies masked the antiseptic hospital odors.

Samantha was the only visitor left in the room. She'd pulled her chair up next to Rachel's bed and was whispering something in her ear when we walked in.

Rachel was lying in the bed, propped up with several pillows. There was an IV drip attached to her arm, and unidentifiable machines surrounded her. An uneaten dinner lay abandoned on the tray. She smiled when she saw us standing in the doorway.

I smiled back, but the sight of her made me want to cry. In the few days since I'd last seen her, her appearance had deteriorated. Rachel was naturally slender, but she'd lost weight she couldn't afford to lose. She looked ghastly, like one of the consumptive patients from Rose's science books. Her skin and lips were so pale she looked as though she'd been drained of blood. Her skin was almost translucent. The white streak in her hair had grown so wide it almost covered the entire crown of her head, which made her look my grandma's age.

She was barely recognizable as the Rachel we knew. It was as if the beauty had been sucked right out of her.

I focused my gaze on Samantha. "Where have you been?" she snapped.

"The nurse wouldn't let us come in," I said. "Too many visitors." I smiled at Rachel. "It seems you're as popular as ever."

Samantha frowned but didn't say anything else.

"I have had a lot of visitors," Rachel said in a weak voice. "Miss Foster, Nurse Phillips, and some of the other teachers from school stopped by." She saw the flowers, which lay forgotten in my hands. "Are those for me?"

When I nodded, she looked delighted. "They're lovely. Everyone has been so nice." She gestured toward the entire greenhouse of bouquets already in her room. That's when I saw the ankh bracelet on her thin wrist.

I said to Rachel, "I like your bracelet."

"Samantha gave it to me. Isn't it great?"

"Peachy," I said, narrowing my eyes at Samantha.

"Rachel is still part of the squad, Daisy," she said. "We're all wearing them." She looked pointedly at my wrist. "Everyone, it seems, except you."

"I forgot it at home," I said. I'm a terrible liar.

Sam glared at me.

Rachel looked distressed at our bickering, and I felt ashamed of myself about arguing in a hospital room.

"Next time we visit, we'll bring magazines," Poppy promised, just as I opened my mouth to apologize.

"Rachel's going to be out of here in no time," Samantha said. "Isn't that right, Rach?"

Rachel said weakly, "Yeah, sure." But she didn't sound very convinced. After a long silence, she added, "Poppy, magazines would be very thoughtful. I honestly don't know how long I'll be in here."

Time to do a little digging. "Has your doctor narrowed it down at all?"

Samantha changed the subject abruptly. "Did I tell you who the newest couple is?" She sent me death rays with her eyes, but I ignored the warning.

Rachel ignored Samantha's lame attempt at avoidance. "The doctors are stumped, Daisy," she said softly, "and it's getting worse." A tear ran down her cheek, but she smiled at me and I could see a glimmer of remaining beauty.

Samantha turned away, but not before I saw that she was weeping silently. And my normally chatty sister was completely silent.

As soon as I could speak, I said, "We'll do anything we can to help you. Anything."

Rachel's mom arrived, toting a big Tupperware container of food. "I hope you have an appetite tonight," she said to Rachel, "because I made all your favorites." She added, "She doesn't like the hospital food, and I can't say I blame her."

"We'd better go," I said. "Rachel, I'll see you soon."

I told Samantha I was riding home with Poppy and we said good-bye.

In the car on the way home, I dug through my purse, looking for a scrap of paper to write on, when the paper towel I'd scribbled on earlier fell out.

"What's that?" Poppy pointed to it.

"I jotted down a few notes from Rachel's chart, but I can't

understand it," I admitted. A thought occurred to me. "Do we have time to stop at the library? Maybe we can find a medical dictionary."

As we left the hospital parking lot, a mint-condition pink 1957 Thunderbird convertible squealed out of the driveway and cut Poppy off as she started to make the turn. Poppy slammed on her brakes, and the driver honked her horn and sped past us.

"Learn to drive," Poppy shouted, but we were both a little shaken by the incident.

"It was a beautiful car, though," I said. "Dad would have loved it." My father had loved classic cars.

"Maybe not in pink," Poppy giggled. She sobered quickly and said, "I haven't heard you talk about Dad in a long time."

"I didn't have anything to say," I replied. My father had been a professor at UC Nightshade until his mysterious disappearance five years ago. The official version is that he died while doing some research in a forest in northern California. The unofficial version, which was talked about in hushed whispers all around town, was that he ran off with another woman, leaving behind his wife and three daughters.

My mother refused to believe either version and preferred to think he was still out there somewhere—alive, but unable to get back to us. This is one case where her psychic powers were useless. I think he just left us and never looked back. And that's why I never talked about my father.

"Mom's still looking for him, you know," Poppy said. "All

those nights when she says she's working late? I think she's still trying to find Dad."

"Mom's a hopeless romantic," I said.

Poppy said softly, "Hopeful, Daisy. She's a hopeful romantic."

I didn't know how Mom could still have hope after all these years. I know I didn't. I just wanted to survive my junior year.

CHAPTER ELEVEN

That Friday evening, there was no football game, so I went with the rest of the squad to visit Rachel in the hospital again. Poppy came along to deliver the magazines she promised. Unfortunately, Rachel wasn't doing any better. Poppy and I left the hospital saddened by her dire state.

Things seemed pretty grim between Ryan and me, too. We had planned to hang out that night, but for some reason he had never called.

"I need a pick-me-up," I said. "Want to go to Slim's?"

"Sounds good," said Poppy. "Why don't you call Rose and see if she wants to come along."

Rose was just getting out of her last class of the week when I reached her on her cell phone. She said she'd meet us at the diner.

Hanging with my sisters at the diner was way better than sitting home on a Friday night. A lot of Nightshade kids drove to Santa Cruz and hung out at the pier on the weekends, which meant Main Street was usually dead on Friday night. Tonight was no exception.

At Slim's, Flo sat at the counter, thumbing through a magazine. When we entered, the bell over the door jangled. I assumed its purpose was to alert Flo to the presence of customers, but it certainly didn't interrupt her reading.

Rose was already waiting for Poppy and me in our favorite booth, the one at the end by the big bay window.

Flo eventually meandered over to take our order. Tonight her shirt read, "I LIKE CHILDREN—FRIED."—W.C. FIELDS.

"I'm starving," Poppy said. "This was a great idea, Daisy. Comfort food is just what we need." She ordered a plate of chili fries and a chicken sandwich. Rose tried to order a salad, but we convinced her she needed a side of onion rings, too.

"Is there fresh coffee, Flo?" I asked. "I need coffee and a cheeseburger."

Flo ambled off to put in our order and then resumed her position at the counter.

"Coffee?" Rose said. "At this time of night? You'll never get to sleep." It was seven o'clock, tops.

"I won't be able to sleep anyway," I confessed gloomily. "I want to help Rachel, but I don't know how." I had been to the library a few times that week trying to interpret the information I had copied from Rachel's chart, but it was no use. I didn't even understand half of what I'd read.

"Oh, the sick cheerleader," Rose said. "How is she doing?"

"We went to see her again today," Poppy said. "She looked like she's at death's door."

"The doctors have run all sorts of tests and found nothing," I said. "Or at least that's what they're telling Rachel."

I sighed. I had been so determined to figure out Rachel's problem myself, but who was I kidding? Rose studied science at college, so she had a much better understanding of medical jargon than I did.

I dug through my purse, found the paper towel with my notes on it, and handed it to Rose. "Maybe this says different."

Rose looked over my notes. "Daisy, I won't ask you how you got this information," she said.

"Good. And I won't tell you," I replied.

She studied the scribbles for a few minutes.

"Well?" asked Poppy anxiously.

Rose shook her head. "They haven't been able to diagnose her with anything. They're stumped. Either Rachel's faking it or—"

"Or what?" Poppy and I said together.

"Or it's not natural at all. I think what's happening to Rachel is supernatural, and the best hospital in the world can't cure that."

"We do know that there's a psionic vampire in town," Poppy said. "What you heard at the council meeting confirmed it."

"How do we trap a supernatural villain?" I said.

We stared at each other. It was a question that none of us had an answer for.

I sighed and put my hands in my pockets. I was wearing the hoodie I'd worn the night Ryan and I snuck into the morgue. The night he'd kissed me for the first time.

My hand touched something metal—the bracelet Samantha had given me. I pulled it out of my pocket and laid it on the table.

"Rachel had on a bracelet just like that," Poppy observed.

"Samantha gave them to all the girls on the squad," I said. "I don't like wearing it, though. It gives me the creeps. The ankh has a connection to vampirism. Right, Rose?"

"It can also represent life," Rose said skeptically.

I looked at the bracelet, more confused then ever.

"Are you saying you think Samantha Devereaux is the psionic vampire?" Poppy asked under her breath.

"Sometimes I think she could be," I admitted. "What if she's using these bracelets as some kind of energy conductor or something? She's always making sure we're wearing them. Maybe they help her get her soul fix."

Rose and Poppy looked doubtful.

"The vamp has to be someone who has access to the cheerleaders," I continued. "She's the head cheerleader, so she definitely has the opportunity."

"But what's her motivation?" Rose asked.

"I don't know," I said. "Beauty? Popularity?"

"Samantha's always been beautiful," Rose replied.

"Plus, she's already the most popular girl in school," Poppy pointed out. "And she's only a junior!"

I finally gave up. I couldn't even convince my own sisters that Samantha could be our vamp. "Well, who else could it be?" I asked, but nobody had any answers.

Flo finally arrived with our food. I bit into my deliciously greasy cheeseburger.

Rose picked daintily at her salad, but I noticed she slathered the onion rings with barbeque sauce and ranch dressing.

I glanced out the window and noticed a couple walking toward the police station. There was something about the back of the guy that looked familiar. Long legs, broad shoulders, and a few rebellious curls caressing the back of his neck. It was Ryan. With another girl. I couldn't tell who she was, but she wore a black cowboy hat.

I pushed away my cheeseburger. I wasn't hungry any longer. But I was pretty pissed off. It looked like Ryan was taking some other girl to the morgue. From what Officer Denton had said, it wasn't the first time.

Flo pulled up a stool. "Nothing better to do tonight than hang out here?" she said.

Poppy replied, through a mouthful of chili fries, "This is it. What's new with you?"

Flo thought for a minute. "I got nothin'." She snapped her

fingers. "Wait a minute!" She fished a quarter out of her pocket and handed it to me. "Go play the jukebox."

"It's still here? I assumed Slim would have traded it in by now." I wasn't really concentrating on the conversation, but instead stared out the window and willed Ryan to reappear.

Flo shrugged. "It kind of grows on you. Some people like not knowing what it'll play next. Although it doesn't do it for everybody."

It had worked for me before, so I figured it would do it again. Besides, you know what they say, music soothes the jealous girlfriend. So I got up, put a quarter in, and looked at the selections. "Flo, I've never heard of half of these songs."

I selected an old Green Day song but was prepared when a different song came on instead.

"Is this thing defective?" Poppy asked.

"Nope," Flo said. "I'm pretty sure it's doing it on purpose."

"What's the name of this song?" I asked Flo.

"This song is 'Heartbreaker' by Pat Benatar. It seems to be trying to tell you something."

Great. Now even inanimate objects were sending me mixed messages. The last thing I needed to hear was a song about a guy breaking some girl's heart.

The bell above the door jangled, and then Ryan walked in with a gorgeous redheaded girl. This time, I heard the jukebox's message loud and clear.

CHAPTER TWELVE

Ryan and his companion were so engrossed in their conversation that they walked right by our booth before he saw us.

"Daisy, what are you doing here?" Ryan asked. I'd never noticed how shifty his green eyes were.

"Having dinner with my sisters," I said icily. "Heartbreaker" faded and then cut out.

"Oh," he said. "I thought you'd be out with the other cheerleaders."

"I'm not," I stated the obvious. Coldly.

"Oh," he said again.

Oh, indeed.

"You're Daisy?" the redhead squealed. Not exactly the greeting I was expecting. I gave Ryan a puzzled look.

"Oh, thank you, thank you, thank you!" she said. She slid into the booth and threw her arms around me.

"For what?" I asked. Giving her my guy, not drop-kicking her across town, what?

"For saving my life," she said.

"Daisy, this is Cassandra Morris," Ryan said.

Cassandra? Why did her voice sound so familiar? Then I remembered the voice echoing in my mind.

"The girl you saved at the Black Opal," Cassandra chirped.

I thought Rose flinched when she mentioned the name of the club, but I couldn't be sure because Cassandra was bouncing in her seat.

I introduced her to my sisters and then called out, "Flo, can we get a couple more menus, please?"

To Cassandra I said, "Order anything you'd like. My treat." This technique was called greasing the witness. Cassandra ordered a banana split and a Coke. Ryan asked for coffee.

"Cassandra was just released from the hospital, so she was down at the station answering a few questions for my dad," Ryan said pointedly.

Interesting that Cassandra was already out of the hospital but Rachel was still stuck there, growing weaker day by day. Which meant that the vampire, whoever it was, was still feeding off Rachel. Who'd been to the hospital to see her? Practically everybody at Nightshade High.

Then I realized Ryan was still standing, so we all scooted over to make room for him. He sat across from me, next to Rose. He tried to catch my eye, but I ignored him. He wasn't completely off the hook yet. Lead or not, Cassandra was still a gorgeous redhead.

I waited until they'd placed their order and Flo was out of earshot.

"Can you tell us what happened that night?" I asked.

"You sound just like Chief Mendez," she said. "Side Effects May Vary is my favorite band," Cassandra explained. "I never miss a gig. Unless I have a tournament or something."

"Tournament?" Poppy said.

"I'm a cheerleader for the San Carlos Squids."

Poppy made a face at the name. "Who wants to be the *Squids?*" she said.

"Nightshade High doesn't exactly have the best mascot in the world," I said. "We're the Sea Monsters, remember?"

"And UC Nightshade's mascot is the Slug," Rose added.

"So you were at the Black Opal to see the band?" I prompted, trying to bring the conversation back to the night in question.

"Were you alone or did you have a date?" Poppy asked.

"I went alone," Cassandra said. "I like to keep my options open." She elbowed me in the ribs, just in case I didn't get it.

"And is that what you were doing that night? Keeping your options open?" I sounded a little sour.

"Trying," she said with a mischievous glint in her eye, "but there weren't many likely prospects."

"Then what happened?" Ryan asked.

"Well, the band took a break and I went down the hall. I was going to try to sneak backstage and meet them," she explained.

"How did you know where to go to get backstage?" Rose asked.

Cassandra giggled. "This guy I know works there. We've hooked up a couple of times and he told me."

Rose didn't say a word, but I knew she was wondering if the guy was Nicholas.

"Then what happened?" I asked.

Cassandra thought for a moment. "I don't really remember much after that. I think I saw a white light or something and then *bam*, I woke up in the hospital."

She took off her cowboy hat and fanned herself with it. That's when I saw it. There was a long white streak in her hair, just like the one Rachel had.

I nudged Poppy, who asked Cassandra, "Did you get your hair highlighted recently?"

Cassandra looked puzzled. "No, but what does that have to do with anything?"

"Maybe nothing, but maybe something," I replied. "Do you know where you got that streak of white in your hair?"

"Not a clue," she said indifferently. "I like it, though," she said. "It makes me stand out from my twin."

"You have a twin?"

"Yes, her name is Chelsea," Cassandra said. "We're not identical, but we look enough alike that people still get us confused sometimes."

Chelsea? Chelsea Morris, the dead girl from the morgue, was Cassandra's sister? Oh, no. I knew there was something familiar about Cassandra besides the voice and the cowboy hat.

I exchanged a glance with my sisters. Should we break the bad news to Cassandra? It didn't seem right to keep the information from her, but it would sound absolutely crazy to tell someone that her dead sister was running around Nightshade. Oh, and we thought she was a psi-vamp.

"Maybe we could talk to your sister," Rose suggested.

"I haven't talked to her lately. She's staying with our dad right now in Los Angeles. She and my mom got into this huge fight," she said.

I grabbed a napkin and wrote down my name, phone number, and e-mail address. "If she gets in touch with you, have her call or e-mail me, okay?" I had a dreadful feeling we wouldn't be hearing from Chelsea. I hoped I was wrong. I hoped it was like in the movies. Maybe if we found the head vampire before Chelsea sucked the life out of someone, it wouldn't be too late for her.

Cassandra shrugged and put the napkin in her purse. "Sure, but she's pretty mad at Mom. Chelsea hasn't even been returning my phone calls."

Ryan looked at his watch. "I should get Cassandra home."

"Why?" she said. "I don't have to be home for ages. I thought we could go somewhere and talk."

Poppy rolled her eyes at that one. I could almost hear her thinking, *What an obvious line.*

"You don't have to be home," he said, "but I do. Daisy, are you ready to go?" His eyes pleaded with me to say yes. Since I didn't want Ryan to be stuck fending off Cassandra's advances, or even worse, *not* fending them off, I said yes.

We made it to the door before Poppy called out, "Be good, kids!"

Ryan and I both blushed. Cassandra looked from Ryan to me and said, "So you two are a couple, I guess." She sounded disappointed.

Ryan grabbed my hand and held on for dear life. "Yeah, we're a couple," he said. It was news to me. Dating, yes, but to me, *couple* meant something more. I just hoped it meant the same thing to Ryan as it did to me.

We dropped Cassandra off at her house, which was a cute little bungalow in the pricey part of San Carlos.

"Maybe I'll see you around at the Black Opal," she said. "Side Effects is playing another gig next weekend."

"You're going back to the club after what happened to you?"

"Sure, my dad always says you gotta get back on the horse, you know." She tilted her cowboy hat at a rakish angle. "Thanks again for everything."

"Cassandra," I called as she walked to her front door, "do me a favor and don't go anywhere alone, okay?"

"Will do," she said.

We watched from the car to make sure Cassandra made it inside safely, and then Ryan drove me home.

This time, he parked away from the streetlight and cut the engine. And when he kissed me, I didn't worry anymore about vampires, or beautiful redheads, because his kiss told me everything I needed to know.

CHAPTER THIRTEEN

That week, I didn't make much progress with the psionic vampire case. But in my defense, Samantha scheduled practice every single night after school, which definitely cut into my sleuthing time.

By Friday, every muscle in my body ached. It had been a long time since gymnastics. So I had to repress a groan when Samantha announced that we'd have a Saturday-morning practice as well.

"Bright and early," she said. "I expect everyone to be there."

"But we have an away game tonight," I protested. "We won't be back until late."

"Suck it up, Giordano," she said. "You need to toughen up if you're going to be a cheerleader."

Miss Foster smiled at me sympathetically but didn't override Sam's order.

"You're doing a great job, Daisy!" she said.

It was a drag to practice on Saturdays, but the football team practiced then, too, so I was looking forward to hanging out with Ryan afterward.

But I never even saw him after practice. I loitered outside the boys' locker room, but he never showed. Finally, I started feeling like a football groupie, so I gave up and walked home alone.

As I left the school, a car pulled up and honked its horn. "Hey, Daisy," Jordan called from the driver's seat, "do you need a ride?"

"No thanks, Jordan," I said. "I'll just walk, it's no biggie." I wanted some time alone to mull over the case.

I still liked being alone more than the average Nightshade cheerleader, but it was nice to know I had options. The old Daisy would have *had* to walk home by herself. Now I had friends. The thought made me smile the entire way home.

As soon as I got in the house, I checked the machine to see if there were any calls. There weren't. Evidently, having a boyfriend was suspiciously similar to *not* having a boyfriend, but I refused to sit around moping.

I went into the kitchen and inspected the cupboards. I felt like cooking something special. The kitchen was completely stocked, for a change.

In the living room Rose was studying as usual, while Poppy painted her toenails and watched television.

"I thought I'd make calzones if everyone will be home tonight," I announced. "And maybe we can rent a movie."

I looked at Rose, but Poppy answered. "I was going to go out with Candy, but her grandparents are in town. A night in sounds good, especially if it includes calzones."

"Maybe I'll make a tiramisu, too," I said, peeking at Rose. Tiramisu was her favorite. The book she was reading concealed her expression, but I thought I detected a twinkle in her eyes.

"Mom will be back from Grandma's in a little while," Poppy said. Mom usually spent Saturday afternoons with Grandma Giordano. "I'm sure she'll be glad to have dinner ready when she gets home."

"Great," I said, restraining myself from pointing out to Poppy that she never made dinner for Mom or anyone else. "You and Rose can go to the video store while I cook."

"Maybe we can rent *An American Werewolf in London*," Rose said as she and Poppy left. It was her favorite movie, and now I knew why.

I decided to make the tiramisu while the calzone dough rose. After I soaked the ladyfingers, I whipped up fresh cream and shaved a slab of dark chocolate. I put everything together in a trifle bowl and put it in the fridge to set.

The bread dough for the calzones was ready. I checked the clock—5:00 P.M. and Mom still wasn't back from Grandma Giordano's—*if* that's even where she'd been. I wasn't sure about anything since Poppy revealed her suspicion that Mom was still trying to find out what had really happened to Dad.

The phone rang right when I was kneading the dough. I grabbed it with one gooey hand.

"Hello?"

"Daisy, it's Samantha." Perfect timing. And what did she want now?

"Can I call you back? I'm in the middle of something."

"Is Ryan there?" she asked. "Is that why you're busy?" She put a particular emphasis on busy. She had a dirty mind.

"I'm cooking, Sam," I said. "Ryan's not here." I wasn't going to tell her I had no idea where Ryan was. It wasn't like we were glued at the hip or anything.

"Then I'm coming over," she said.

"But . . ." Dial tone.

I was surprised at how fast Samantha got to my house. Right after I finished the dough, I heard a car pull up. I peeked out the window and saw Samantha's cute little BMW convertible in the driveway.

I didn't give her time to ring the doorbell. She was already standing on the stoop, carrying a bag of groceries. Her hair was in a ponytail and she wore black designer sweats with pink trim. If DEAD was stamped on her butt, I was so going to kick her out of my house. Instead, her butt read DIVINE in pink letters.

"What's so urgent?"

"Daisy, are you going to invite me in or what?" Hmm. Did she *need* to be invited in? Sounded vampy to me.

"You don't need an invitation," I said. I watched her closely, but she just pushed through the front door and headed for the kitchen.

I trailed after her. She put the groceries on the counter and took an appreciative sniff. "It smells great in here. What are you making?"

"Calzones." Samantha used to love those, back when we used to be friends.

"Oh, fabulous! I'm starving." Starving? I thought cheerleaders didn't eat. Except me, which explained why I wasn't going to be climbing to the top of the pyramid any time soon.

I stared at her. "Samantha, what are you doing here?"

For a minute, her bright expression dimmed. I had sounded harsh. "I mean," I hastily continued, "it's Saturday night. Don't you have a date with Sean?"

"Oh, I told him I needed a girls' night out."

"What are you and the rest of the squad going to do?" Samantha only hung with other cheerleaders.

"I thought I'd hang with you tonight."

"Me?" I was surprised.

"You *are* a cheerleader, Daisy," she reminded me.

Oh, yeah. But not a *real* cheerleader. I had only joined the squad to investigate. Even so, I was kind of having fun.

"But I'm hanging out with my sisters at home tonight. Movies and junk food. Not very exciting."

"It sounds perfect to me," she said. "I brought ice cream." She gestured to the brown paper sack.

"I'm making a tiramisu," I said, and then realized my reply

sounded less than gracious. "It's Rose's favorite, but Poppy loves ice cream."

Samantha looked around the kitchen. "Where are they?" she asked.

"Video store," I said. "Rose wants to see *An American Werewolf in London.*"

"That's still her favorite?" Samantha asked.

"She always did have a thing for the furry ones," I said.

We both giggled and our eyes met, both of us remembering how we used to be friends. Part of me was hoping we could be again, but I wasn't going to admit it to Samantha, at least not until I knew if I could trust her.

"I'd better finish preparing the food," I said. I took the calzone fillings out of the fridge and started to grate the cheese.

"Can I help?"

"It's really a one-person job." And I had no idea what to talk to her about.

"Why don't you pick out some music?" I pointed to the small player on the kitchen counter. "We can use this, but most of the CDs are in the living room."

"I'll go get them," she said.

I expected her to choose some trendy dance music, but she didn't. Instead, she put an oldies compilation into the CD player.

"Remember this song?" she said. "Your parents used to dance to it in the kitchen."

I snapped the stereo off. "That was a long time ago."

"I didn't mean . . ." She trailed off, and I was surprised to see tears in her eyes. "Daisy, I'm sorry. I'm sorry for everything I did that year, everything I said."

"Why'd you do it, Sam? Why did you tell everyone that my dad left my mom for another woman?"

"Because I thought it was true." Our eyes were locked, which is why I didn't realize my mom was home until I heard her long shaky breath.

Could it be possible that my mother had never heard the rumors? That she really didn't have a clue?

The look on her face told me she had heard every rumor but that she didn't expect me to believe any of them. And now she knew I did.

CHAPTER FOURTEEN

Samantha realized it, too. "I guess I should be going now," she said, after one look at my mother's stricken face.

Mom seemed to gather herself together, but there were purple shadows under her eyes. A visit to Grandma Giordano's didn't make her look like that.

"Oh, Samantha, don't go!" she said. "We'd love to have you stay for dinner, wouldn't we, Daisy?" Mom looked at me expectantly.

"Yeah, don't go, Sam," I said. "We were going to watch a movie, remember?" I was shocked that the words came out of my mouth.

"If you're sure?" Samantha asked, looking up at my mother.

Mom smiled at her warmly. "It's nice to see you back here, Samantha. And you're welcome anytime."

"Thanks, Mrs. Giordano. Why don't I set the table?"

"That would be very nice," Mom said, "but maybe you'd like to call your parents first?"

"They're out of town this weekend," Samantha replied quickly. "I'm home alone."

"Why don't you spend the night?" Mom suggested. "We'd love to have you whenever your parents are away." I gave Samantha a don't-get-any-ideas look.

"Mom, why don't you go put your feet up? I'll make you a cup of tea."

"I think I will," she said. "It's been a long week." She wandered into the living room while I put the kettle on.

Samantha stood watching me for a moment. "Is everything still in the same place?"

"Mom's rearranged things a bit," I said. I showed her where we kept the silverware and napkins.

I put a little honey in the tea and added a splash of milk before taking it to Mom.

"Thanks, Daisy," she said. She watched me for a moment, then said, "It's not true, you know."

"What's not true?"

"Your father didn't leave us for another woman. He was working on something—something secret—when he disappeared."

"You think his disappearance had something to do with his work?"

She nodded. "I had no idea you'd heard those awful rumors," she said gently. "You were so close to him. I know it was hard for you, but don't ever doubt that your father loved us. You especially."

"If he loved us so much, why is he gone?" The question burst out of me.

"I don't know, Daisy," she said. "But I know that if it was within his power, your father would be here with us right now."

"That's not what the rest of the town thinks."

"Is that why you stopped being friends with Samantha? I'm glad to see you've made up."

I stared at her. "Samantha was the one who *started* the rumors, Mom, so don't think that she and I will start being best buds again."

"Daisy, go easy on Samantha," she said. "Things haven't been easy for her."

I ignored her last comment. Mom had always had a soft spot for Samantha. But I was still focusing on what she'd said about Dad. "So where do you think he is?"

Mom's smile faded. "I don't know, Daisy, but I'll find out."

I didn't say anything else. I grabbed an afghan from the couch and put it over her shoulders. "Why don't you rest? We'll have dinner as soon as Poppy and Rose get back."

"I am a little tired," she admitted. "A nap sounds good." Her eyes were already closing as I tiptoed out of the room.

I checked on the calzones and then went to find Samantha. She'd finished setting the table and was standing motionless, staring at a spot on the wall. She looked alone.

"All finished here?" I said. I felt like I was interrupting or something.

"I don't have to spend the night," she said. "It was nice of your mom to invite me, but I can leave after dinner, if you want."

"No, that's okay," I said. "I want you to stay." I was surprised to realize it was true. "Are your parents traveling?"

She nodded. "Dad's work again. You know how it goes." Samantha's father was a professor at the same college where my father had worked. In fact, they had done research together—research that Mr. Devereaux had published to great acclaim after my father disappeared.

Poppy and Rose came through the front door. "Are you ready for a movie marathon?" Poppy called out.

At the sound of my sister's voice, Samantha looked strangely self-conscious, like she wasn't sure of my sisters' welcome.

Poppy walked into the dining room. "Is dinner ready yet? I'm starving." Then she caught sight of Samantha. "Oh, hi there. I didn't know we had company."

"Samantha's spending the night," I explained.

Rose appeared in the doorway. "Good," she said. "After dinner, we'll make popcorn and watch the movies."

"Sam brought ice cream," I said. "And I made tiramisu. You want popcorn, too?"

"Sure," Rose replied. "What's a girls' night in without junk food?"

The timer buzzed. "Speaking of junk food," I said. "I need to take out the calzone before it burns."

Poppy came to help me carry the food into the dining room,

and then we sat down to eat. My mom looked better after her nap and even had a glass of red wine with dinner.

After the food had been passed around, Poppy said, "Where's Ryan tonight, Daisy?"

"I have no idea," I admitted.

"Why the sudden interest in Ryan Mendez's activities?" Mom asked.

For the first time, I was glad my mom's psychic abilities had limitations.

"Daisy and Ryan are dating," Poppy blurted out.

My mom reacted quite calmly to the news. "I wondered about that. I know I've been so busy with work lately, but the chief mentioned to me that you and Ryan have been spending a lot of time together."

She changed the subject quickly, to my relief. I didn't want my love life to become the topic of dinner conversation.

"Samantha, Daisy tells me you're the captain of the cheerleading squad. Are you enjoying it?"

Samantha chattered away about the upcoming homecoming game, but I only listened with half an ear. What *was* Ryan doing tonight, anyway? And why hadn't he called me? Oh, no. Clingy girlfriend alert. I decided to concentrate on having fun with my family and Samantha, and tuned back in to the conversation.

After we'd stuffed ourselves silly, we moved to the family room for DVDs and dessert. Mom headed to bed, but not before she'd had a big helping of tiramisu.

I was glad Mom had stayed awake long enough to eat dinner. I hadn't seen much of her lately. And her smile had been missing even longer, at least the kind of smile she gave us tonight, the kind that actually reached her eyes.

Rose snagged *An American Werewolf in London* and popped it into the DVD player. Poppy and I had seen it a million times, and she had to keep hushing us as we talked over it, but Samantha was as enthralled as Rose.

The movie was almost over when the doorbell rang. "Are you expecting company?" I asked and got negatives in reply.

I went to answer it and found Ryan on my doorstep. He had a nasty-looking gash above one eye.

"Ryan, what happened?" He swayed a little and I realized I hadn't asked him in.

"Come on." I took him by the arm, just in case he fainted or something. He was looking a little green.

"You don't look too good, Ryan," Poppy said when we entered the living room.

Rose looked him over and clicked off the movie. "Get the first-aid kit, Poppy," she said.

"No, it's okay," Ryan assured us. "I've already been to see the school nurse. This cut isn't as deep as it looks."

Rose looked doubtful.

"Is your dad home tonight?" Poppy asked.

Ryan shook his head. "He's helping with a case over in San

Carlos. Nurse said I shouldn't drive until tomorrow, so I walked over here."

"You can sleep here," Rose offered. "On the couch," she added, just in case he was getting any ideas. From the sickly look on his face, I didn't think ravishing me was the first thing on his mind. "Someone needs to check on you, just in case you have a concussion."

"Now tell us what happened!" Poppy said.

"I was at the library at school," Ryan started, but Samantha interrupted him.

"On a Saturday?" she said disbelievingly.

"I was doing research," Ryan said, "about . . . my family. But I'd just found something that might help with your investigation. I had it in my hands and then, suddenly, everything went black." He stared at his hands for a moment.

Was Ryan trying to contact his mother? Everyone knew that she'd left Ryan and his dad and lived in San Francisco with her new boyfriend. It was one of the things we had in common.

"When did this happen?" I asked.

"After football practice," he said. "Luckily, Sean came looking for me to get a ride home. I think he scared off whoever it was."

"Why didn't he take you to the hospital?"

"I wouldn't let him," Ryan said. "I'm fine." He swayed as he said it. I rolled my eyes. Guys, always trying to act tough. "Honestly, Daisy, I'm fine," Ryan reassured me. "We ran into Nurse Phillips on the way out of school and she cleaned me up. She even kept an eye on me for a few hours until she was sure I was okay to go."

"Do you think someone was following you?" Rose asked.

"Maybe," Ryan said. "I don't know why else someone would bash me in the head, unless I had something he or she wanted. When I woke up, it was gone."

"What was gone?" I asked.

"The newspaper clipping. The one I wanted to show you. It was a photo of a woman who looks exactly like your cheerleading coach. And the caption identified her as Hannah Foster."

"A photo of Miss Foster?" It may have been all the carbs, but I was having a hard time following him.

"So?" Poppy said what we were all thinking. "What's the big deal about a photo?"

"So the photo was *old*," Ryan emphasized. "From 1958, to be exact. There was an article too, but I didn't get a chance to read it before I was hit on the head."

I said, "Didn't anybody see anything? That's pretty daring to attack you in the open like that."

Ryan said, "I was in the back, where they keep all the old files."

"What were you looking for when you found the article?" I asked.

"I was looking for information about the history of Nightshade," he said. "For a school project," he added quickly. Hmm. Earlier he had said he'd been doing research on his family. Was Ryan trying to find out if his father was part of the council?

"Maybe the article was about Miss Foster's mother?" Samantha suggested.

"Grandmother would be more like it," Rose said.

"But if the woman was in her early thirties fifty years ago," I said, "she'd be over eighty by now."

"What's the big deal?" Samantha said. "It could be a relative of hers. Everyone says I look exactly like my Aunt Nancy. Besides, Foster is a common name."

"But if it's *not* a big deal, then why was Ryan hit on the head and the article taken?" I said.

There was silence as everyone absorbed the latest.

Samantha said, "You do have a point, Daisy."

"What if something was keeping her young?" Rose suggested.

"You mean like plastic surgery? There's not enough plastic surgery in the world," Poppy said.

"Not plastic surgery," I said slowly, finally understanding where Rose was going with it. "Something else. Something supernatural."

I shot my sisters a look of warning. I didn't want to reveal too much about the psionic vampire situation in front of Samantha. At this point, it seemed like the Divine Devereaux was innocent of any soul sucking, but I still had a nagging feeling that there was something she wasn't telling us. I looked over at her, curled up in the corner of the couch. Was that her normal couldn't-care-less expression, or did I detect a flash of worry in her eyes?

CHAPTER FIFTEEN

Sunday morning, I started down the stairs and then remembered that Ryan had spent the night on the couch. I went back up to brush my teeth and hair and put on some vanilla-scented lotion before I tiptoed into the living room.

What did he look like when he slept? I crept closer, only to find an empty couch. The blanket was folded, the pillows neatly stacked, but there was no sign of Ryan.

I told myself that he left early so his dad wouldn't worry, but I was miffed. I had left a brief message for Chief Mendez explaining the situation. Ryan could have stuck around for pancakes, at least. It felt like he was deliberately avoiding me. Boys were so complicated sometimes.

I wanted to complain to Samantha, but she was still asleep in the other twin bed in my room. I went back to bed, pulled the covers over my head, and went back to sleep.

Two hours later, I was up again and late for cheerleading practice. Samantha was already long gone. Miss Foster was going to kill me. But really, what kind of monster schedules practice on a Sunday? Sunday was supposed to be downtime. No homework, no school, no extra-curricular activities.

Instead of lounging, I was stuck hanging out with a bunch of cheerleaders, shaking my groove thing and trying not to snap when Samantha ordered me around.

Samantha had been less obnoxious than usual lately, but that didn't mean she wouldn't take her role as head cheerleader as seriously as, oh, say, Attila the Hun.

I got to the gym and lined up in formation next to Penny Edwards. She flinched when she saw me, which reminded me I'd accidentally stomped on her foot during the dance routine at the last practice. Penny had been to the salon, I'd noticed. It was hard not to. Her hair had so many white stripes in it that it resembled a barber's pole.

I thought of Rachel's hair and Cassandra's. And Chelsea's. They all had streaks, too. Was Penny the victim of a vampire or just a victim of fashion? It was hard to tell. If the popular girls had stripes in their hair, Penny would have stripes in her hair.

When I looked around, I realized the entire squad (except me, of course) was dressed in black. I looked closer and saw that they weren't entirely in black; they also wore blood red ribbons in their hair. I tugged on my dingy gray sweats and hoped Samantha wouldn't notice that I obviously hadn't gotten the dress-like-a-clone memo.

"Daisy, you're late," Samantha barked. "And what are you wearing? Where's your practice uniform?"

I sighed. It was like last night had never happened. When Sam put on a cheerleading uniform, good Sam disappeared and the Divine Devereaux, her evil twin, appeared.

Miss Foster came over and I marveled at how . . . peppy she looked. Entirely too perky to be someone's well-preserved grand-mother. In the light of day, my suspicions about my gym teacher seemed ludicrous.

She was carrying a neatly folded bundle of clothing, which she handed to me. "It's my fault, I'm afraid. I forgot to give Daisy her new practice uniform."

Samantha frowned. "I suppose we can take a five-minute break while Daisy makes herself decent."

The rest of the squad walked off the floor while I glared at Samantha's back.

Miss Foster followed my glare. "Beauty has its price," she said softly. "It's not easy being the best, the prettiest. Sometimes, sac-rifices have to be made."

Something in her voice was giving me serious heebie-jeebies. I stared at her, but all I saw was a woman whose own beauty was slowly fading. I saw fine wrinkles at the corners of her eyes. Mom called them laugh lines, but Grandma Giordano called them crow's feet. I wondered exactly how old Miss Foster was.

Somehow, my suspicions were back. I wished I had seen the article Ryan had found with my own eyes.

"I'd better go get changed," I said. The locker room was empty when I entered. As I dressed, I felt like someone was watching me. "Hello?" I called. There wasn't a sound. I shrugged, feeling foolish, but still changed into the black sweats as quickly as I could. I crammed my clothes into my bag and headed back to the gym.

When I got there, the gym was in chaos. Trina Manahan was writhing on the floor. A clump of girls stood over her, wringing their hands. Jordan was having hysterics in the corner.

As I watched, Samantha strode over and shoved Penny Edwards aside. "Give her some room," she said "Penny, call 9-1-1. She's having a seizure."

Penny gasped, but whipped out her cell phone and punched in the numbers. As I watched in shock, Trina's body jerked and her arm flailed out. I noticed she wasn't wearing her bracelet.

"Daisy, go get Nurse Phillips!" Samantha said.

I wasn't much better. I just stood there, my mind unable to process what was happening. "But it's Sunday."

"She was just in here talking to Trina less than five minutes ago. Now go!"

I ran down the hall toward the nurse's office.

Nurse Phillips wasn't in her office, but from the heavy scent of hairspray, she'd been there recently. I followed the trail of Aqua Net at a jog. I turned the corner and nearly collided with her. I didn't recognize her at first because she was missing her usual beehive and white uniform. Instead, her blond hair was in pigtails and she wore a T-shirt and jeans.

"Trina," I panted. "Seizure. Gym."

She took off at a run. She was a pretty good sprinter, and I had a hard time keeping up with her.

We heard the sirens as we entered the gym. Trina had stopped convulsing but was unconscious. Someone had covered her with a spirit blanket and there was a balled-up varsity jacket under her head. Dread crept over me. As I watched Trina, a thick white line appeared in her shiny black hair.

Stunned, I studied the room while Nurse Phillips bent down and took Trina's pulse. Samantha knelt on Trina's other side and whispered words of comfort. At least I hoped they were comforting words and not "Get up! You're a cheerleader."

Trina could end up just like Rachel or, worse, like the dead girl in the morgue. I saw something gleaming from the floor. Her ankh bracelet. It must have fallen off while she was stretching.

Trina's best friend, Alyssa Garfinkle, started sobbing. Everyone's attention swung to her. Nurse Phillips was still doing something to Trina.

My hand inched closer and I hooked a finger on the bracelet. I glanced around. No one was looking. I slipped the bracelet into my pocket.

A couple of minutes later, the paramedics arrived and Samantha and I got out of their way and sat on the bleachers. I flashed back to the club. It was a frighteningly similar scene. As they wheeled Trina out, Ryan rushed into the gym, dressed in a sweat-stained T-shirt and shorts.

Relief crossed his face when he saw me. "Daisy, what happened?"

After I explained things, I asked, "What are you doing here, anyway?"

"Lifting weights," he replied. "Coach wants me to bulk up a little."

"Is Sean here?" Samantha asked.

"Nah," Ryan said. "He decided to sleep in. Wyatt's spotting me."

I noticed Ryan wouldn't look me in the eye. Ever since that night at the diner with Cassandra, he'd been so distant. Sure, we were both busy with practice, but you'd think he'd make some time for me. Even last night when he came over, he admitted it was only because Nurse Phillips told him not to drive. Something was definitely wrong, but I had other things to worry about. There was a monster on the loose, one who seemed to be targeting the Nightshade High cheer squad.

The parents started to come by to pick up the girls. I looked on as the gym began to empty of hysterical cheerleaders and their equally hysterical parents.

"I heard it was a drug overdose," Alyssa's mom said in a horrified whisper. She should know a thing or two about that, since rumor has it that Alyssa just got out of rehab last summer.

"I heard she has anorexia," Nicole's stepdad insisted.

"Cutting," Mari Lopez's mom said. "I read an article about it."

It wasn't any of those typical nightmares for parents: pregnancy, pills, or pain. It was something worse. For a second, I thought about saying it out loud—telling everyone that it was the vampire.

Which meant that the vampire had been here, right under my nose. Who had been near Trina? I glanced at Samantha, who was at the other end of the bleachers filing her nails with a bored expression on her face. The pendant gleamed from her neck. Why was she the only one who rated a pendant? Everyone else had bracelets.

"Daisy?" I realized that Ryan was staring at me expectantly. I'd zoned out and missed half of the conversation.

"Sorry," I said. "My mind was somewhere else. What did you say?"

"I asked you if you wanted to grab a coffee at the diner," Ryan said. He sounded serious.

He wouldn't break up with me at the *diner*, would he? He knew it was my favorite place.

I glanced over at Samantha, who was studiously pretending not to listen to our conversation. She'd been a pain lately, but Ryan wouldn't break up with me in front of an audience.

"Can I invite Samantha?" I said.

He sighed audibly, but nodded.

"Daisy, what are you doing?" she hissed as I walked over. "He wants to be alone with you."

"I don't want to be alone with him," I said in a whisper. "Please come with. I'll totally owe you."

There was a knowing look on her face. "I was nervous with Sean, too. Just don't let Ryan push you into anything you're not ready for," she said. "Of course I'll go, but you're going to have to be alone with him eventually."

What was Samantha talking about? It was like we were having two completely different conversations. It didn't matter, as long as she came along.

"I'm inviting Sean," she said, already taking out her cell.

"The more the merrier," I said. I smiled in satisfaction. *Try breaking up with me now, Ryan Mendez,* I thought. But breaking up was the last thing on his mind.

CHAPTER SIXTEEN

We rode to the diner in Ryan's car. Samantha chattered away on her cell phone, but Ryan and I were quiet.

Part of me knew it was unreasonable (okay, crazy) to assume that he was going to break up with me, but I had issues. Disappearing dad, remember? And as my mother had painfully reminded me, I had been Dad's favorite. Look where that got me.

Slim's was packed. Half the cheerleading squad was in a booth in the rear of the restaurant. Miss Foster sat in the middle.

Sean was already there, holding a table for us. He must have broken land speed records to get to the diner ahead of us. Ryan immediately went to join him.

Jordan waved us over. "Samantha, over here!"

"Hi, Sam. Hi, Daisy," Penny chirped. "Miss Foster decided to take us out for lunch."

"I thought the girls could use a little treat after that upsetting incident," Miss Foster said. "Won't you join us?"

Penny kicked Jordan in the leg in her eagerness to make room for Samantha. Jordan gave her a dirty look.

"No thanks," Samantha said. "Sean has a table for us already." She gave him a little wave, and he practically bounced in his seat when he saw her.

I followed Sam back to the booth. "I ordered you an extra-large coffee with cream and sugar, one splash of vanilla syrup," Ryan said.

Just the way I liked it. I smiled at him as I slid into the booth. I couldn't help it. He was just so cute.

I said, "Remind me to thank you later"—before I realized that it might have sounded ever so slightly suggestive, at least from the curious way Samantha was looking from me to Ryan.

It wasn't what I meant. At least I didn't think it was.

From the way Ryan smiled, it hadn't occurred to him, either. I relaxed and leaned into the curve of his arm.

"Are you hungry?" he asked.

And even though the place was packed, Flo was there in a twinkling to take our order.

"Starving," I said. I ignored Samantha's tiny headshake. Ryan and I had been friends way before we started dating. It wasn't news to him that I liked to eat. I ordered a cheeseburger and fries.

With a shrug, Samantha said, "I'll take the same. Make it rare. As bloody as possible."

Sean looked at her like she'd grown a second head.

"Is there a problem?" Samantha asked him coldly.

"No, no," Sean said. "It's great. It's just, I've never seen you order anything but salad."

"I'm ordering it now." She smiled at me. "It sounded delicious."

I wondered why Samantha was in such a good mood, especially after what had happened to Trina. I also wanted to know why she hadn't bothered to wake me up to get to practice on time, since she had spent the night at my house. Did she have something to take care of and didn't want me to interfere?

"So, did I miss anything before I got to practice today?" I asked her. "How did Trina look when she showed up?"

"Not good," said Samantha. "In fact, Miss Foster took her to Nurse Phillips's office when she first arrived."

"Nurse Phillips?" I repeated, alarmed. I had dragged Rachel to see the nurse the day Rachel collapsed in gym, and she was still down for the count. I was getting an idea and I didn't like it.

"Yes," Sam said, "she wasn't feeling well, but Trina didn't have a fever or anything so Nurse Phillips okayed her to practice. Miss Foster made sure she drank a whole bottle of water before we started."

I looked over at Miss Foster in her booth across the diner. She chatted happily with the other cheerleaders. Maybe I had been wrong in suspecting her. Maybe the picture Ryan saw had been a fluke—after all, he had taken a blow to the head that day. If Miss Foster really was the vamp, she would have had ample opportunity to take out the entire squad by now.

But Nurse Phillips had plenty of opportunities, too. Trina had been to see her only minutes before she had her seizure. What was the motive? She was a nurse, someone sworn to save lives, not take them. But then I remembered the headlines I'd seen about nurses who killed their patients, and I wasn't so sure. Was Nurse Phillips a cold-blooded killer?

The jukebox suddenly kicked on again. I hadn't noticed anyone feeding it quarters, but I wasn't exactly surprised.

"Evil Woman" was the song of choice. Was it trying to tell me something?

I decided I'd feed it a few coins and see if it changed its tune. I dropped them in the slot and punched a few random selections—B5, C10, and A1—and waited to see what happened.

"Evil Woman" cycled through again. It *was* trying to tell me something. If I took it literally, there was an evil woman somewhere on the premises. Unless it thought I was an evil woman for lusting after Ryan so obviously.

I passed by a large table and noticed Nurse Phillips herself was sitting there with a bunch of people.

I waved at her as I passed, but she called my name. "Daisy, come meet some friends of mine."

"Evil Woman" cut off in the middle of the song and was replaced by "Rock 'n' Roll High School" by the Ramones. The last time I heard that song was at the Black Opal. What was that possessed pile of tin trying to tell me?

"This is Camille." She pointed to a brunette in her thirties who was trying to pass for a fan girl of fifteen. "Bert," a skinny guy with a goatee and a streak of red running through his hair, and "Vinnie," a short dark-haired guy wearing a Speed Racer T-shirt.

"Hey, what about me?" the remaining guy said.

Nurse Phillips sighed. "And this is Jeffrey," she said.

Jeffrey was a short, stocky blond with rings on every finger and a large mole on his nose. I shook hands with him.

"Are you a fan?" he said. He slipped me a piece of paper. His hand was damp and oily. I wiped my hand on the back of my jeans, under the pretext of putting the paper in my pocket. I just hoped it wasn't his phone number.

"Uh, yeah, big fan," I said, having no idea what he was talking about.

"You should come see us sometime," Jeffrey leered.

"Knock it off, Jeff," Nurse Phillips said sharply. "She's one of my students."

Penny came up and stood right in front of me. "Nurse Phillips, can I have your autograph now? I know you said not to bother you at school, but we're not in school now."

"Autograph?" I said stupidly. I was obviously missing something.

Which Penny was happy to make clear to me. "You've got to be kidding me," she scoffed. She flipped her skunk-striped hair. "You don't know? Nurse Phillips is the bass player for Side Effects May Vary."

"I had no idea." I stared at Nurse Phillips. That meant she was at the Black Opal the night Cassandra was attacked.

"Figures," Penny snorted.

"It's okay, Daisy," Nurse Phillips said. She smiled at me. "Penny exaggerates our popularity. Some of the kids at school found out I was in the band."

"You mean, everyone who is anyone," Penny said under her breath.

"I'd better get back to my friends anyhow. Nice to meet you." I was missing something. I knew it.

I fished out the piece of paper Jeff had given me and saw that it wasn't his phone number, but a flyer for Side Effects May Vary.

When I got back to the table, Samantha and Sean weren't there, which gave me a chance to tell Ryan my new theory.

I waved the flyer in front of Ryan's face. "Nurse Phillips!" I said. "It has to be her."

"What do you mean?"

"The vampire," I said. "I think the vamp is Nurse Phillips. She was there every time a girl was attacked."

"So were you and Samantha," Ryan pointed out.

"So?" I said, feeling irritated that he'd been keeping track of Sam's whereabouts.

"So there were plenty of people around," he said. "You, me, Sam, Sean, Nurse Phillips. Half the cheerleading squad was at the club that night. That doesn't mean any of them is the vampire."

"It doesn't mean one of them isn't," I said.

"Besides, I thought vampires couldn't go out during the day, and Nurse Phillips is at school every single day."

"That's just a myth," I said. "Besides, we're looking for a soul sucker, not a blood sucker."

"True," he said.

"Hey, you spent a few hours with her yesterday," I said. "Did you notice anything vampy about her?"

"No," Ryan said, "but I was a little woozy." Suddenly, he cleared his throat. "I wanted to ask you something." He hesitated while I imagined the worst.

"Go on," I said.

"Would you go to the homecoming dance with me?"

I smiled at him. "I'd love to." Now I felt woozy.

A few minutes later, when I came back to Earth, I realized that Sam and Sean still hadn't returned.

"Where'd they go?" I asked Ryan.

He said, "They're outside. Fighting."

"But their food will get cold," I said.

"They'll be back in a minute," he said. He slid an arm around my waist and pulled me closer. He kissed me gently on the lips.

I hesitated. My mind was whirling, but from the way Ryan was kissing me, he didn't want to break up.

Oh. Oh. *Oh*. It finally sunk in what Samantha had been talking about earlier. She had thought I didn't want to be alone with Ryan. But I did. I did want to be alone with Ryan. Just maybe not *alone* alone. Not yet anyway.

I was so absorbed in thoughts of being alone with Ryan and the homecoming dance that I almost missed Nurse Phillips. She was in the parking lot saying good-bye to her band mates, about to make her getaway. I grabbed Ryan and we followed her.

We trailed Nurse Phillips to a tiny cemetery just outside town. Ryan pulled through the gate and parked the car down the lane, under the shelter of a couple of large trees.

"What do you think she's doing here?" I asked Ryan. We could see her from the car. She walked along the rows of headstones until she found the one she was looking for and stayed there for a long time.

"Whatever it is," he said, "she's not looking for her next victim. These people are already dead."

I punched him on the arm. "That's not funny. What if she's waiting for her fledgling to rise?"

"We should wait until she leaves and look for fresh graves," Ryan said. Although slightly repulsed by the idea, we did as he suggested.

After she drove off, I hopped out of the car. "You take that row and I'll take this one."

"Why don't we stay together?"

"Good idea," I replied.

We drew closer to the approximate location where she'd been.

I didn't see any fresh graves, but I did see something that made me stop in my tracks.

One of the headstones was carved with a familiar name. It read "Christian Phillips, beloved husband." The dates on the stone made it clear that it was probably Nurse Phillips's husband.

"She was just visiting a loved one," I said. I pointed to the fresh bouquet of flowers on the granite.

As we walked back to the car, I said, "Did you see any stones marked with the Foster name?"

"No, but we didn't get very far."

The newspaper article Ryan found had been from the *Nightshade Gazette*, which meant there was a good chance that the woman in the picture would have been buried here.

"Let's check. Remember that photo? Maybe we can find Miss Foster's relative here."

Or maybe not. Although we spent over an hour combing the cemetery, there was no sign of any Fosters.

I was certain that she was our vamp, but how was I going to prove it?

CHAPTER SEVENTEEN

The weeks leading up to homecoming were tense. Samantha had all the cheerleaders jumping around, painting posters, hanging banners, and making "spirit boxes" for the football players. One day, the cheerleaders actually drove to In-N-Out and brought back about a hundred double-double cheeseburgers for the football team's lunch.

With all the preparations, I didn't have much time to focus on the vamp problem.

One Thursday after school, I went shopping with Poppy and Rose. They helped me pick out the perfect dress for the dance. It was deep midnight blue, silky to the touch, and fit me like nothing else I'd ever owned. I couldn't wait for Ryan to see me in it.

I was floating until we got home. Then I hit the ground with a thump.

Mom met us at the door. "Daisy, can you make something a little special for dinner tonight?"

"Sure, but what's the occasion?"

"I've invited Chief Mendez and Ryan for dinner," she said.

My sisters stifled their laughter.

"I told them seven-thirty. I hope that will be all right?"

Unbelievable. "Fine," I said.

She said, "Great. I've got to finish some work, but holler if you need anything." Mom wandered upstairs with a file in her hand.

As soon as she left, Rose said, "What was she thinking?"

"Dinner with the parents already?" Poppy said. "It's the kiss of death."

"We've had dinner with them before," I reminded her.

"Yeah, but that was *before* you two were dating," she said.

"What am I supposed to do?" I looked at my watch. "It's too late to cancel."

"You have to talk to her," Rose said.

"I'll talk to her later. I'll have to make the best of it for now."

"If it's any help," Rose said, "Mom gave me a list and I went grocery shopping earlier today, so we're all stocked up."

"That's a huge help," I said. "But I'd better get started."

I rushed to the kitchen and checked to see what Rose had bought, then rifled through my cookbooks. I had no idea what to make. Potluck would not do for a dinner with the parents. I had to make something special, in order to distract them. They'd be so full from stuffing themselves that they'd forget to ask any awkward questions.

What did guys like to eat? I thought frantically. Meat. Men liked to eat meat, right? Ryan wasn't a vegetarian and neither was the chief. I opened the fridge door and stared in. I spied a large beef roast in the back and grabbed it.

I'd make pot roast. I checked my watch again. I had just enough time to cook it, as long as I served munchies first.

I hated cooking under pressure, which is one reason I'd never make it as a professional chef.

I checked the oven to make sure Poppy hadn't stored anything inside. I'd never forget the time I accidentally set fire to her school project, which she'd left in the oven to dry. As the oven preheated, I went over my mental checklist. I'd make a quick salad.

I wished I had more time to prepare, but there was no sense in wringing my hands about it. When I turned around, a gorgeous salad sat in a big wooden bowl on the counter.

I frowned. How had it gotten there? Rose or Poppy must have made it, but when? It looked good, but it was missing shredded cheese. I was headed for the fridge when the refrigerator door opened and a package of shredded cheese floated out and to the counter, where it hovered uncertainly, as if waiting for further directions.

I did not have time for my sister's pranks. "Poppy," I called out. "Cut it out. I don't have time for this." There was no answer. "Poppy," I yelled it this time.

She walked into the kitchen a few seconds later. "You bellowed?"

I gestured toward the cheese, which still hung in midair.

"I'm stressed enough about making dinner for Ryan and his dad, so quit it, okay?" I said.

"I'm not doing it," she said mildly.

"Then who is?" I put my hands on my hips and glared at her.

"You are," she said. That's when the package of cheese exploded.

CHAPTER **EIGHTEEN**

After the bag exploded, showering us with mozzarella, Poppy started screaming with excitement. "Mom, come here! You're never going to believe it! Daisy's . . ."

Mom came running. "For heaven's sakes," she said. "What's wrong?"

"Nothing's wrong," Poppy started to explain, but I gave her a pleading look and shook my head the tiniest bit, hoping that Mom wouldn't notice.

"Er, um, Daisy's . . ." Poppy's imitation of a guppy was quite remarkable.

"I wanted to know if we had any fresh garlic," I improvised wildly. "I'm going to make stuffed mushrooms."

"Is that all?" Mom put a hand to her chest. "You almost gave me a heart attack. Look in the pantry."

"For what?" I asked.

My mom glanced at Poppy and then back to me. "Are you girls sure you're all right? You're both acting very strangely."

"We're fine, Mom," I said. "I'm just . . ." I sent Poppy a wild look. Help! I wasn't ready to deal with my newfound powers, if that's what was happening. I definitely wasn't ready to tell Mom, not until I knew my psychic powers were here to stay. I didn't want her to get all excited only to find that I was a norm after all.

"Nervous about cooking dinner for Ryan," Poppy said quickly. "Why don't you go to the living room and relax? I'll bring you an appetizer when they're ready."

"If you're sure you don't need anything else, I will," Mom said, still looking confused. "I still have work to do."

"Thanks for not saying anything," I said to Poppy, after Mom left.

"No problem," she said, "but I don't get it. Don't you *want* to be psychic?"

"I don't know," I admitted. "I'm used to the idea that I was a norm. It never occurred to me that I could be anything else." It was also something I shared with my father. And now it seemed that was gone, too.

"But you are," Poppy said. "You're one of us now."

"Meaning I wasn't before?" I replied. She didn't know how much her words hurt, since they only confirmed what I'd always suspected. That I was an outsider in my own family.

"I didn't mean . . ." Poppy trailed off uncertainly.

"I know you didn't," I said. "Can we keep this between the two of us?"

"You mean not even tell Rose?" Poppy looked shocked.

"If she picks up on it, we'll tell her," I decided. "Otherwise, no."

Poppy still looked doubtful, so I added. "Just until I know it wasn't some kind of fluke. There's no sense in getting everyone excited when I don't even know if I can do it again."

"Try while you're making dinner," Poppy said.

"I don't know what to do," I admitted.

"What were you doing when it happened?"

"Fixing dinner."

"No, I mean what were you feeling? What were you thinking about?"

"I don't know. It just happened. How does it work when you do it?"

Poppy thought about it. "When my powers manifested, I couldn't control them. Mom told me to take a deep breath and then tell the object to move."

"Let me get the mushrooms in the oven first," I said. "Then I'll try."

I was nervous about failing. Turns out I had a reason to be.

First I tried to float the dishes into the dishwasher. No luck. Then I tried something smaller, an orange from the bowl of fruit on the counter. I tried and tried while I finished up with dinner, but nothing happened.

The timer went off and I bent down to check the food. "See, it was a fluke," I said. I was grateful that I could hide my face. I didn't want Poppy to see how upset I was. I took a deep breath and tried to convince myself that I was relieved I didn't have any powers.

After a minute or two of pretending to study the oven's contents intently, I took the mushrooms out. The roast was still cooking. The kitchen clock told me I had just enough time to change before Ryan and his dad arrived.

The doorbell rang just as I finished applying lipstick. They were early. Was that a good sign, as in *I can't wait to see Daisy,* or a bad sign, as in *I can't wait to get this done and over with?*

At dinner, Chief Mendez complimented me so effusively that both Ryan and I were blushing.

"You'll make someone a great—" *Don't say it!*

There was the distinct sound of Ryan's shoe connecting with his dad's shin.

"—chef someday," Ryan's dad continued blandly.

Poppy giggled madly, but Rose glared at her and she finally stopped.

Dinner concluded without any more inappropriate comments, much to my relief.

"Why don't you girls show Ryan the living room? Pete and I will clean up," Mom said. "There's something I want to talk to him about anyway."

"Ryan's seen the living room before, Mom," Poppy said dryly.

"C'mon, Poppy," Rose said, "You heard Mom."

Ryan started to take his plate into the kitchen, but Mom took it from him and shooed him off.

Ryan and I loitered in the hallway, out of their range of vision. He took my hand. "Was that weird or what?"

"The weirdest," I agreed. "What do you think they're talking about?"

"Probably a case they're working on," Ryan said. He pulled me closer.

Reluctantly, I put a hand out to stop him. "What if that's not what they're talking about?"

"Daisy, you worry too much," he replied. "Besides, what else could it be?"

"Us."

That one word galvanized him into action. He put a finger to his lips and led me back to just out of sight from the kitchen, still holding my hand. I could hear my mother's voice, but not what they were saying.

I moved closer, brushing against Ryan as I passed. My heart sped up but then slowed almost to a stop when I heard what my mother said next.

"I don't think we should do anything. Let the council handle it."

Ryan's dad said something I didn't catch.

Then my mom's voice came through loud and clear. "I can just see the county coroner's face when we tell them that the dead girl was spotted at Slim's Diner tonight."

Ryan pulled me closer and gazed into my eyes. "Are you okay? You look pale."

"I'm fine, really," I said. But I wasn't fine. Samantha Devereaux's phony dead girl act aside, it made me queasy to think of a real dead girl, poor Chelsea Morris, hanging out at my favorite spot and stalking unsuspecting customers. "Let's go talk to my sisters."

They were in the living room. "What are we going to do?" Poppy asked after I told her what we'd overheard.

"I have an idea," I said. "Ryan and I will go look for the girl. Rose, can you call Nicholas and see if he knows anything?"

"All right, Daisy, but I'm not sure he'd tell me even if he did know anything," she said. There was a trace of bitterness in her voice.

"Is everything okay between the two of you?" I asked.

"It's okay," she said. "I just don't want to talk about it right now."

Poppy said, "It doesn't seem fair. What do I get to do?"

"Stay home and cover for us," I said.

"What should I tell them?"

"Tell them we went to get some ice cream for the dessert. But stall as long as you can!"

"What's for dessert?" Poppy asked, diverted by the mention of food.

"Brownies," I said. "Now do you think you can cover for us?"

"I'll think of something." I didn't like the mischievous look on her face, but there wasn't anything I could do about it now.

"Thanks," I said as we left. "And save me some brownies."

Slim's was empty, except for a couple making out in the corner booth. I couldn't tell who the girl was, because she wore a baggy black sweatshirt with the hood pulled up, which obscured her face and hair. I recognized Bane Paxton, though, a senior at Nightshade, and if rumors were correct, a complete dog when it came to the opposite sex. He had a dopey expression on his face, which made me assume that the date was going well, at least by Bane's standards.

Ryan ordered a quart of mint chocolate chip—Poppy's favorite—while I moved to get a better look at Bane and his date. It was the baby vamp all right. Chelsea looked like a fledgling bird with her mouth open. She seemed to be trying to inhale Bane, but he took it as a signal to move even closer.

I started forward to warn him when there was a loud thud. Flo and Ryan froze as I dashed toward Bane, who was convulsing on the ground.

Flo grabbed the phone and dialed 9-1-1.

The baby vamp pushed past me and almost knocked me over as she bolted for the door.

"Stop her!" I said, but she was already gone. "Where'd she go?" I looked through the big bay window, but the street seemed empty.

Out of the corner of my eye, I caught a glimpse of movement. I dashed out the door. I ran down Main Street in the direction I thought I'd seen something.

I heard Ryan's footsteps behind me, but I didn't slow down. I could see the figure of the girl up ahead. She was running now, too, and her hood fell down to reveal long red hair.

She turned the corner and headed toward a residential area.

I followed, acutely aware that I was gasping for breath. Ryan was close to catching up to me, but I couldn't wait. The girl was only a few yards ahead of me now.

"Daisy!" Ryan hollered. "Do you realize we're following someone who could kill us?"

"We've got to see where she's going," I gasped. "You heard what they said at the council meeting. The fledgling can lead us to the vampire."

We were in an older section of Nightshade. Oak trees flanked the street and the houses sat back from the sidewalk as if they wanted nothing to do with the street.

She reached a row of neatly kept houses and veered quickly, changing directions.

"Chelsea! We can help you," I hollered.

"Nobody can help me," she shouted. She cut through a yard and hopped a six-foot fence with ease.

The stitch in my side stopped me. There was no way I could have caught her now, even if I had the superhuman strength needed to hop a six-foot fence like I was hopping over a jump rope.

I was bent over trying to remember how to breathe when Ryan caught up with me.

"Where'd she go?"

Still too winded to speak, I pointed.

Ryan started to take off after her, but I stopped him. "Too . . . late," I wheezed.

A porch light came on and a figure appeared in the door. "Who is out there? What's going on?" I couldn't see her clearly, but the woman's voice sounded elderly, quavering, and fearful.

The figure moved to the front porch and peered at us.

She came down the stairs, and that's when I recognized her. "Daisy, is that you?" I swear the woman's voice changed, became lighter, more lilting somehow. It was Miss Foster, my gym teacher and cheer coach. "What are you doing here this time of night?"

"Just taking a walk, Miss Foster," I said. I hoped she couldn't see the sweat streaming from my forehead. "Sorry to have disturbed you."

Before she could reach us, I grabbed Ryan's hand and headed back the way we came.

"There's a mint-condition pink '57 T-bird in her driveway," I said.

Ryan looked at me admiringly. "You know a lot about cars."

"Just that model," I said. "My dad always wanted one. Not necessarily a pink one, of course. But that's not the point. The point is, Poppy and I saw that same car leaving the hospital when we went to visit Rachel."

"I've never seen it at school," Ryan said.

"Maybe she saves it for special occasions," I said darkly. "Like when she's sucking the souls out of innocent victims."

I was positive now that Miss Foster was our vamp. But I couldn't go to the city council armed only with suspicions. I had a feeling they'd stake first and ask questions later, and I didn't want to be responsible for an innocent woman's death. No, I had to find proof that Miss Foster was our vamp and I needed to find it soon.

When we got back to Slim's, the ambulance had already left.

"How is he?" Ryan asked Flo.

She shrugged. "They wouldn't tell me much," she said, "but they did say that it was lucky I called 9-1-1 when I did. A few minutes later and he would have died."

She handed Ryan a quart of ice cream. "Here you go. The other one melted."

There was still a sticky puddle on the floor where Ryan had dropped the ice cream to chase after me.

"Flo, do you remember anything about the girl who was with him before he collapsed?"

She thought about it for a minute. "Not really. Although I did notice her tattoo. A tiny four-leaf clover on her hand," she replied.

"Thanks, that's helpful." It was our dead girl, I was sure of it. I wandered over to the booth where Bane and Chelsea had been earlier. Nothing there. Not a clue about where she'd gone or what she was doing at Slim's, besides making bad dating choices. I wanted to bang my head against the table, I was so frustrated.

My cell rang. I thought about ignoring it, but I could see it was my sister.

"You've got to get back here now," Poppy said in a low voice. "Mom's going ballistic. I sorta implied something. I didn't know Mom would freak. I'm really sorry. I had to come up with something."

I started to ask her what was up, but she had already clicked off.

Chief Mendez and Mom were waiting for us outside by the time we got back.

"Don't say a word, young lady," she said, practically the second we got out of the car. "You are in so much trouble." I glanced at her face and knew she spoke the truth. Mom was pissed, but about what?

"For going to get ice cream?" I said, truly puzzled.

"You've been gone over an hour," Mom said. "Don't tell me it takes that long to get ice cream. We know exactly what you two have been doing and it's going to stop."

I felt the heat creeping up my face and refused to look at Ryan. Either my mom had an exceptionally suspicious mind or Poppy had royally screwed things up this time. What was really weird is that I'd never seen Mom act like that before, not even when she'd caught the usually saintly Rose breaking curfew with Nicholas Bone when she was a junior.

"But Mom—" I tried to get in a word.

"You're grounded," she said, "and that's final."

Ryan had been studying his sneakers intently, but when

Mom said that, his head snapped up and he finally looked me in the eyes. I could tell he was nearly as embarrassed as I was, but he forged ahead anyway. We couldn't miss homecoming.

"Ms. Giordano, Daisy and I weren't doing . . . anything wrong," he said. "We were at Slim's when Bane Paxton had a seizure. Flo called 9-1-1 and everything."

"Oh," Mom said. She was silent for a moment. "Oh, I'm so embarrassed. Daisy, I apologize for jumping to conclusions. When Poppy said . . . I naturally assumed . . ." She trailed off uncertainly.

For a second, I thought about blurting out that Ryan and I knew all about the psionic vampire they were chasing down, so they would stop treating us like children and whispering about it behind closed doors. But I took a deep breath and remembered that Ryan's dad was probably in the council, and those guys seemed capable of doing some serious damage. I needed to stick to the original plan of cold, hard proof on Miss Foster before I went to the authorities. And that included my mom.

"Let's go inside and have dessert," Ryan suggested, "before the ice cream melts any more than it already has."

I wondered to myself what in the heck Poppy had said to get Mom so fired up. Whatever it was, I needed to make sure to avoid any mention of it in the future.

CHAPTER NINETEEN

Finally, Saturday arrived. The big homecoming game. I stood there on the field shivering in my cheerleading uniform. Despite the cold, Samantha looked radiant.

I had never been a huge fan of football before, but one look at Ryan in his football jersey and I was hooked. After about a month on the cheerleading squad, I had finally figured out some basics. Sean threw the ball, Ryan caught the ball, and Wyatt Pearson tackled anyone who got in their way.

Truthfully, I'd never even been to a football game before becoming a cheerleader. Still, I felt a secret thrill when Ryan ran forty-five yards for a touchdown. The crowd roared its approval.

I turned to Sam. "That's good, right?"

Penny smirked, but Sam smiled. "That's *great*, Daisy," she said.

I did a triple cartwheel and then ended with splits.

We were playing the San Carlos Squids, and we absolutely clobbered them. The game ended with a 21–14 victory for the Sea Monsters.

After the game, the cheerleaders hustled to Samantha's house to prepare for the dance. The Devereaux house was palatial by Nightshade standards. I had been there tons of times back in middle school. But this time, something was different. Like a significant lack of furniture.

The Devereauxs' great room was a hugely imposing space that used to be decorated with leather sofas, oriental rugs, and enormous mahogany bookcases. The room seemed even bigger without the bookcases. The walls were faded in the places where paintings used to hang.

"We're redecorating," Samantha said. "Now, quit gawking so we can get busy."

She led us all upstairs to get ready. I noticed with amusement that her bedroom, unlike her wardrobe, hadn't changed. It was still frilly and pink.

"I don't know why they have to have the dance the same night as the game," Penny complained. "It doesn't give us enough time to get ready." She seemed so low energy lately. Even though we weren't the best of friends, I still worried her soul was slowly being drained by the vamp. If she had a soul, that is. She hadn't shown much evidence of one.

"It's tradition," Samantha said. "So the players have something to look forward to if they lose."

"Fortunately, we won," I said. "But a slow dance isn't much of a consolation."

"So says the innocent," Samantha said knowingly.

As I pulled on my dress, I listened to the other girls chattering about the night ahead. It made me nervous. I wondered what Ryan expected.

"How are you and Wyatt getting along?" Mari Lopez asked Jordan as they applied their makeup in Samantha's vanity mirror.

"All right," Jordan answered indifferently. She giggled and added, "But he has more hands than an octopus."

"Slug him," I suggested.

"What for?" she said, staring at me vacantly.

Samantha offered to do my hair and makeup. Since she always looked like she was ready for a formal dance, I figured she'd do a better job than I would. An hour later, I had been poked, prodded, and powdered into perfection. Or at least as close to perfection as I was going to get. Samantha had tamed my unruly hair into a crown of curls and did my makeup with an expert hand.

"Wow," I said when I saw my reflection. "Thanks, Samantha."

"Don't mention it," she said. "I can't wait to see Ryan's face when he sees you."

"What time is it?" Penny asked, shaking a bottle of black nail polish. "Do I have time to redo my manicure?"

"Not unless that's the quick-drying stuff," said Alyssa, glancing down at her wristwatch. "The guys will be here to pick us up in an hour."

"Alyssa," Samantha said, "why aren't you wearing the bracelet I gave you?"

Alyssa looked sheepish. "Sorry, Samantha, it clashed with my dress."

Samantha surveyed the wrists of the other cheerleaders in the room. I was the only one wearing my ankh bracelet, and truthfully, it was only because I didn't really have any other nice jewelry that would complement my dress.

Samantha became flustered and snappy all over again. "Daisy, can you please stop staring at yourself in the mirror? I've got to put on my own makeup. Why don't you go put on some music?"

She elbowed me out of her way. I put my hands on my hips. "Samantha—" I started to say more, but she interrupted me.

"Please, Daisy, *please* put on some music," she said. "I'm sorry I'm bossing you around. I'm just nervous."

I had no idea what Samantha had to be nervous about. She would surely steal the show when she walked into the homecoming dance in that sexy little black number she was wearing. I walked over to her CD rack and rifled through her collection. I spotted an old Hillary Duff CD, circa sixth grade, that I thought would get a few laughs, at least. Everyone was taking this dance way too seriously.

"Not this, Daisy," Samantha snapped. "If I wanted to listen to kiddie pop, I'd go hang out at the elementary school."

I suppressed a sigh and handed Jordan a stack of music. "Maybe you can find something," I said.

I stormed downstairs. I needed to bang some pots and pans or something. It was either that or strangle our hostess. Samantha could be such a pain sometimes.

I usually cooked when I was upset. And I was upset, but the Devereaux kitchen soothed me. It was amazing, at least to a foodie like me. The kitchen was all granite countertops, maple cupboards, and gleaming stainless-steel appliances.

Too bad there were only a few eggs, some questionable-looking cheese, and a stale loaf of bread in the state-of-the-art fridge. I decided I'd make myself an omelet while the other girls finished their dance preparations. It was better than being bossed around by Samantha upstairs.

I rummaged through the cupboards until I found a mixing bowl and utensils. When I was looking for a spatula, I also found a stack of past-due bills. What were they doing hidden there? The Devereauxs were rich, weren't they? Were they in trouble?

I was puzzling over it when suddenly I spotted something much more interesting poking out from underneath the bills. It was a crumpled photocopy of an old newspaper article. And sure enough, there was the photo. Ryan was right—the woman in the photo looked *exactly* like Miss Foster. My blood ran cold as I slowly realized what this meant. Samantha must have been the one who attacked Ryan for the article. Was she covering for Miss Foster? Or was Sam herself a vamp?

Before I could figure it out, Samantha burst into the kitchen. "Daisy, I just want to apologize—" she started, and then stopped dead when she saw I was holding the article in my hands. "I can explain," she said.

"Well then you'd better start," I said, taking a step back toward the sliding-glass door to the patio in case she was going to take this opportunity to come after me and suck my soul.

"Look, Daisy, I've known for a while there was something weird going on with Miss Foster, and what I heard from you and your sisters and Ryan that night I was at your house just confirmed it," Samantha said. "I left your house early the next morning because I wanted to get to school before her so I could search her office. I found that article crumpled up in her trash can."

I looked at her skeptically. "Then why didn't you tell me? Or someone else? How could you just sit back and continue to let her suck souls?"

"I didn't know exactly what she was doing," Samantha protested. "All I knew is that cheerleaders were getting sick and it seemed to be related to her. But I knew if I told someone I'd just sound crazy, and they'd probably send me to the school therapist again."

"Again?" I hadn't been aware Sam had any mental problems. Attitude problems, maybe.

Sam nodded. "There have been some, um, issues with my family lately," she said. I could tell she didn't want to talk about it. I'd have to grill her about it later. "That's why I just thought it would be better to keep my mouth shut. You and your sisters have each other. You even have psychic powers. You're much better equipped to handle the situation than I am."

I was about to protest that I didn't have psychic powers, but then I remembered what had happened when I was preparing dinner the other night. For now, I'd just hope that wasn't a fluke.

I looked down at the article again. My hands were still shaking. "Well, now that we have proof that Miss Foster is going around attacking people, we have to tell someone," I said.

"How about your mom?" Sam suggested. "She'll know what to do."

I nodded. "She's on her way over here to take pictures of us before the dance. We'll tell her everything then."

Suddenly Sam's eyes widened. "Chelsea?" she said. "What is she doing here?"

I whirled around. There was the baby vamp, standing outside on the Devereaux patio. I flung open the sliding-glass door and approached her slowly.

"Oh, Chelsea," I said. The fear left me and I walked toward her. "I can take you home," I coaxed.

She took a step back and shook her head, but I could see the yearning in her eyes.

"I can help you."

She shook her head again and then vaulted over the fence.

I didn't go after her. I really couldn't have if even I wanted to, not in three-inch heels and an evening gown.

"What on earth was that?" Samantha shrieked.

"I'll explain later," I said. "Right now we have to warn the other girls there's a vampire in the vicinity."

We rushed upstairs. But to my horror, Samantha's bedroom

was empty. Lip glosses and curlers lay scattered about. The cheer-leaders were gone.

I went back downstairs as fast as my dyed-to-match pumps would carry me, with Samantha following close behind. Sure enough, the front door was wide open. I caught up to them at the end of Samantha's driveway. There was a line of cheerleaders walking down the street in the direction of the high school. Some of them were barefoot, and all of them had glazed, unfocused looks in their eyes.

Sam and I fell into step behind the last cheerleader and tried to replicate their vacant stares. Evidently, our destination was the high school. Moonlight cast strange shadows across the big double doors. I took a deep breath and entered after the other girls.

The corridors, which should have been full of people rushing around and preparing for the big dance, were eerily empty. We headed for the gym. It was decorated with streamers and balloons. The girls in front of me lined up like they were getting ready to execute a routine. I fell into formation and waited, my heart beating rapidly, for the vamp to appear.

I started to shiver when I sensed a malignant presence. Then I was slipping into the vampire's mind.

I didn't mean to, but it just happened. Kind of like accidentally bumping into someone else's brain. It was like slipping into a sewer, black and foul. I sensed fear, loneliness, and incredible hunger. Hunger that would never be satisfied.

CHAPTER TWENTY

Sure enough, it was my perky, soul-stealing cheerleading coach. She stood directly in front of the cheerleaders. I barely recognized Miss Foster; her features were so contorted with rage and . . . age.

She looked like she'd aged about a hundred years since I last saw her. She was hunched over and her skin was yellow and as clear as cellophane.

She grabbed Penny Edwards's arm and felt it like she was picking out the best cut of meat at the butcher shop. I tried not to throw up. The rest of the squad stood there like good little lambs.

"Leave them alone!" I shouted.

"Daisy Giordano," the thing hissed. "You have been a thorn in my side."

I stepped closer to the vampire and recognized the smell of Aqua Net, the same scent I'd detected at the club.

"That aerosol smell," I said, "is that a vamp thing?"

"That's a hair-spray thing," Miss Foster replied. "A girl has to look her best."

"You're about a hundred years too late to be a girl," I pointed out.

"That's the joy of being a soul sucker," she said. "Youth and beauty in an everlasting supply." That's why she targeted cheerleaders. Youth and beauty in one convenient package.

"Were Trina and Rachel your victims?" I asked. "I can't figure out how you did that, right in front of everybody."

She chuckled evilly. "It won't help you to find out my little secrets."

I waited. I knew she couldn't resist telling me how much smarter than me she'd been.

As I expected, she talked. "It was easy. A little hypnosis, a little soul-sucking. I just needed a little sip. I waited until you were all busy. She shouldn't have collapsed. Perhaps I was a little . . . enthusiastic. Or she was already weak." She shrugged dismissively.

I gaped at Miss Foster in horror. The girls' souls were about as meaningful as an energy drink to her.

She waved a gnarled claw in the air and pointed to Penny Edwards. Penny moved out of line until she was within arm's reach of Miss Foster. The vamp unhinged her jaw like a snake and began to take great gulps of the wispy vapor of Penny's soul, which was a particularly nasty shade of green.

Miss Foster paused and dropped Penny's still body to the floor. She lay there crumpled and white, like a used Kleenex, but the slight rise and fall of her chest told me she was still alive.

Miss Foster's jaw snapped back into place, and she gave a huge burp. "Excuse me," she said daintily covering her mouth. I watched in amazement as her gnarled hand grew smooth and young again. Her eyes brightened and her skin grew rosy, but there was still a web of lines on her face.

"Ah, that's it," she said. "I needed a little pick-me-up before I really get started." She stared at the line of cheerleaders greedily. "Let's see. Who's next?"

"Why the sudden need for so many souls all at once?"

She smirked at me. "Well, Daisy, as you so tactfully pointed out, I'm no spring chicken anymore. And the older I get, the more souls it takes to maintain my appearance. Plus, it seems I've worn out my welcome in Nightshade. I need something a little extra to tide me over until I get to the next town."

I was betting she knew the council was after her and she wanted to split town before they found her and did away with her themselves.

I needed to do something before she ate the souls of everyone on the squad.

I faced Miss Foster and squared my shoulders. She wasn't going to get away with this, not without a fight, anyway. She was a soul-sucking vampire and I was a sixteen-year-old cheerleader, but I was damned if she was going to suck the life out of all my friends. High school was hard enough.

The girls were all still in the trance. Out of the corner of my eye, I thought I saw Samantha move. I averted my eyes before

Miss Foster noticed, but I saw it again a few minutes later. Samantha was definitely not under the spell like the other girls.

"What about Chelsea, your fledgling?" I demanded, desperately trying to stall Miss Foster before she made her next move.

"Chelsea?"

Miss Foster never could remember names. "The girl you turned? Why did you do that?"

"I had hoped for a companion," she said. "But unfortunately, the chit turned out to be greedy and ungrateful."

"I followed her to your house that night," I said.

"Yes," Miss Foster agreed. "I thought for sure you had finally stumbled on my little secret with your poking around, but apparently not, because I'm still here. Though these cheerleaders won't be for long," she cackled.

"I'm not going to let you get away with this," I warned.

"Daisy, dear, you can't stop me. You're not psychic like your sisters, are you? You're not anything, except a very temporary annoyance."

I tried not to let it get to me, but I was getting really sick of being underestimated. And maybe, just maybe, I wasn't completely without powers.

Miss Foster bent down and rummaged through her gym bag. "Ah, yes, here it is," she said.

Her arm came up holding a heavy object, and before I could react, it connected near my left temple. That's the last thing I remember before everything went black.

When I came to, I was tied to a folding chair, which was placed in the center of the gym. The cheerleading squad was still lined up in perfect formation. Jordan Kelley had a small strand of drool coursing down her chin. I tried to pretend to still be unconscious, but Miss Foster noticed.

"Wake up, sleepyhead," she screeched. "I want you to see what I have in store for you." She stretched a few minutes, like she was warming up for cheerleading practice.

Her jaw unsnapped with a loud popping noise, and then she was sucking the life out of the girls. A sound like the howling of the wind filled the gym.

I strained against my bonds, but I was tied fast. *Rose, where are you? Help!* I screamed it in my mind, hoping against hope that Rose would hear me before it was too late.

Rage bubbled up inside me. I wished desperately for the power to do something, anything. I remembered the tomato exploding, and the bag of cheese floating across the room. Maybe it wasn't just a coincidence. I remembered Poppy's advice. "Don't try so hard. Just feel the object moving across the floor."

Miss Foster's head snapped around, as if sensing I was trying something. I held myself very still and she finally returned to her task.

I wished with all I had that something heavy would squash Miss Foster flat. And then something did.

With a loud groan, a set of bleachers disconnected from its steel track and came skittering across the gymnasium floor.

Miss Foster had her back to me, absorbed in the destruction of souls, and didn't notice the bleachers. I held my breath and hoped that her greediness would keep her distracted long enough. It was my only chance to help my friends.

Just then, Samantha sprang toward Miss Foster and shoved her away from the girls. The bleachers flew into the air and landed with a loud bang on top of our cheerleading coach. There was a piercing scream and then silence.

Samantha came over and untied me. "It's about time, Giordano," she said. "I was wondering if you were ever going to take out the garbage."

"You weren't in her power like the rest?" I asked.

"Nope." She touched the ankh pendant around her neck. "Probably because of this."

"The ankh?"

"That's why I gave everyone ankh bracelets," she said. "I thought it might help protect them. Too bad the other girls didn't wear theirs."

The ankhs had actually protected us. And I almost hadn't worn mine. I shuddered at the thought.

I stood up and rubbed my head. I had one beauty of a headache, but other than that, I seemed to be okay.

Ryan sprinted into the gym, followed quickly by Sean, my sisters, Mom, and Chief Mendez.

Ryan rushed up and cradled me in his arms. "Are you okay?

God, Daisy, I was scared. I went to go pick you up at Sam's. Then your mom and sisters drove by and told me that you needed help. I called my dad right away."

I smiled. Rose must have heard my telepathic cry for help.

"We came as soon as I could figure out where you were," she said. "Next time be more specific when you send a psychic SOS."

"Did you do that?" asked Poppy, pointing to the destroyed bleachers.

"I think so," I said. "Unless it was you?"

Poppy shook her head. "Mom, guess what? Daisy finally got her power! I knew it!"

"Are you okay, honey?" Mom said. She brushed back the hair from my eyes.

"Mom, didn't you hear me?" Poppy said. "Daisy got her power and it's a doozy."

"Yes, yes, I heard," Mom said. "But I'm more concerned with making sure that your sister is all right."

"I'm fine," I said. "And Poppy, I think it's powers, as in the plural. I'm pretty sure, but they seem to come and go."

"That's awesome, Daisy," Poppy said. "I'll help you learn to channel your powers."

"The vamp?" Rose said. "It was Miss Foster, wasn't it?"

I nodded and pointed to the pile of twisted metal, suddenly too tired to speak. We could see two sneakers peeking out of the rubble, just like the witch's shoes in *The Wizard of Oz.*

"You just gave a whole new meaning to the term 'under the bleachers,'" Poppy said. She leaned over and examined the debris. "Eww!" she said. "Gross."

Squashed vamp had an atrocious odor. It smelled like school cafeteria food, the boys' locker room, and a healthy dose of evil.

The rest of the cheerleaders were coming out of their hypnotized state. Penny Edwards came running over. "What happened?" she asked. "The last thing I remember, we were at Samantha's getting ready for the dance."

How were we going to explain this one? Penny wasn't the brightest cheerleader in the bunch, but she had a nose for gossip like a bloodhound's.

"Earthquake," Chief Mendez said, after a long pause.

"Don't you remember?" Samantha said. "Miss Foster called a last-minute practice."

"Oh, yeah," Penny said. "Practice right after the homecoming game." She looked down at her dress. "In our evening gowns."

"I know, what a pain, huh?" I said. "But she was freaking about . . . about tournaments. She thought we needed more practice." She thought we needed the soul sucked right out of us, but Penny didn't need to know that. I shuddered at the memory of Miss Foster's face as she drank from my friends.

"Where is she?" Alyssa asked, looking around the gym. "And why do I feel so strange?"

"Unfortunately," I said, thinking quickly, "a row of bleachers collapsed on her. There was nothing anyone could do."

"No one but you," Ryan whispered in my ear.

I grinned at him. It felt pretty good to save the day, even if most people would never know. I quickly wiped the smile off my face when I realized that the other girls looked horrified. It was easy to forget that they weren't aware of their cheering coach's demonic nature.

"Oh my god," Jordan whimpered. "That could have been one of us!"

"This is awful," Penny wailed. "What about the homecoming dance?"

"I'm sure it will be rescheduled," Samantha assured her.

Chief Mendez spoke briefly into his radio and barked some instructions, then turned to us. "Why don't you girls go on home? Someone will be here soon to clean up."

"Not much left to clean up," Ryan commented.

I shivered. If we hadn't been able to stop her, the gym would have needed a major cleanup. Cheerleader all over the floor.

"I'm starving," I said. My stomach growled.

"Let's go to Slim's," my mom suggested.

Samantha looked hopeful, and several of the girls looked up at the mention of food. So much for cheerleaders never eating. Of course, we had all been through a lot tonight, even if most of them wouldn't remember it.

When we walked into Slim's, the jukebox clicked on "Another One Bites the Dust," a favorite at football stadiums everywhere. I felt like the music was the jukebox's way of giving me a pat on the back. Even more important, I hoped it was telling me that the psionic vampire had indeed bitten the dust.

CHAPTER TWENTY-ONE

The homecoming dance was postponed until the next week. This time we got ready at my house, and there were no interruptions from the undead.

The gym, where we had all our dances, with the exception of prom, had been transformed with red and silver balloons and liberal applications of crepe paper.

Sean and Samantha grabbed a table while Ryan and I headed for the dance floor, which had been set up near the basketball hoop at the far end of the gym.

My head turned whenever I smelled hair spray, but it turned out to be Jordan Kelley's overly enthusiastic use of the stuff to keep her coif in perfect curls.

The whole school was thrilled because Side Effects May Vary was providing the music. As I passed the stage that had been set up for the band, Nurse Phillips winked at me with one glittery false-eyelashed eye and continued strumming her bass guitar.

The chaperones were guarding the punch bowl. Wyatt Pearson was determined to spike it, but I doubt he'd manage to get through my sister Rose, who was chaperoning. I waved to her. She looked incredibly lovely in a soft fuchsia dress.

When Ryan and I reached the dance floor, the tempo of the music changed to a slow dance, and Ryan pulled me into his arms. "Perfect timing," he said.

I nestled closer, content to close my eyes and let him lead me around the dance floor. Even with my eyes closed, though, I could tell that he avoided a stubborn oily stain on the gym floor that was all that was left of Miss Foster. Or at least I hoped it was.

A few minutes later, Cassandra and Chelsea Morris entered the gym on Bane Paxton's arms. Cassandra saw me and waved me over.

When the song ended, Ryan and I headed their way.

"I didn't expect to see you here," I said to Cassandra when we approached her table.

"We couldn't turn down a chance to go to a Nightshade dance," she replied. She gestured to her sister. "This is my sister Chelsea. She came back home last week and she's been dying to meet you!"

The streak of white was gone from Chelsea's hair, and her skin glowed with life.

I met Chelsea's eyes and grinned at her. "I hope not!"

"I don't get it," Cassandra said, perplexed.

"Just a little inside joke," Chelsea replied. "I owe Daisy a lot."

"I didn't know you two knew each other," Cassandra said.

"We don't," her sister replied, "but we do have a lot in common."

We had secrets in common. I don't think Cassandra was ready to learn that her sister had nearly been turned into a psionic vampire. Chelsea looked alive and healthy, which was the important thing.

The other cheerleaders and I were gathered at the punch bowl when Rachel appeared. Everyone started squealing.

Samantha rushed up to her, beaming. "When did you get out of the hospital?"

"Yesterday," she replied, "but my mom made me stay home an extra day. I can't stay out too late, either."

She looked great and healthy again, and the white streak was gone from her hair. I guess killing the vamp really did put the victims back to normal—Mindy Monson, Kelsey Sebastian, and Trina Manahan had all returned to school earlier that week. "Do you remember anything about your episode?" I asked her.

Rachel shivered and wrapped her arms around herself. "I don't know, Daisy. The last thing I remember is you and Ryan helping me to the nurse's office."

I looked at her closely. There was something about the way she had said his name. It dawned on me that Rachel liked Ryan.

"Rachel, I—"

She blushed. "Ry—he's a nice guy."

I met her eyes.

"But he's totally into the girl he's dating now," she said softly. Now it was my turn to blush.

I glanced around the room at the animated faces of the cheerleading squad. The white streaks in their hair were fading. Except for Penny's, which confirmed my suspicion that most of hers had been done at the salon in an effort to be in style.

"I'm going to miss you," I said to them. And I would, even Penny.

"Miss us?" Rachel said. "What do you mean?"

"Everyone is healthy again. The whole squad. So you don't need me any longer."

"Of course we need you," Samantha said. "You can be the alternate's alternate or something."

I smiled at her. We both knew that there wasn't room for me on the squad any longer.

"I'm really going to miss cheerleading."

"You don't have to sound so surprised," Samantha said. "Besides, you'll always be a part of the squad. Once a cheerleader, always a cheerleader."

I couldn't help myself. I reached over and hugged her. And she hugged me back.

A microphone emitted an earsplitting amount of feedback and we all looked up. Principal Amador was onstage, and he spoke into the microphone. "Sorry about that. It's time to announce the Nightshade High homecoming king and queen."

Samantha had it locked, but I was less certain about who

would be crowned king. Adam Zeigler, Poppy's date, was the most popular senior boy, but Ryan was well liked. Sean was another strong candidate, as captain of the football team and Samantha's boyfriend. I'd just decided that Sean and Samantha would win, due to the cute-couple vote, when I heard Principal Amador say Ryan's name.

I was shocked when my name was announced a second later.

Samantha gave me a little shove toward Ryan, who was standing there waiting for me. "Get going, Giordano." I was surprised to see she was grinning widely. I had a sneaking suspicion Samantha Devereaux had a little something to do with my nomination. That girl was seriously good at keeping a secret.

I tucked my arm into Ryan's and we walked to the stage together.

Principal Amador shook hands with Ryan, placed a sparkly tiara on my head, and said, "May I present to the student body Nightshade High's homecoming queen, Daisy Giordano."

The crowd cheered, louder than I expected. Someone gave a piercing whistle, and I knew it came from Poppy. Then I spotted her and Rose in the crowd, both jumping up and down and clapping madly.

Even my mom, who was spending much more time at home now that the case of the disappearing body had been solved, had shown up and was snapping pictures wildly. Sam must have tipped her off. I teared up a little, wishing that my dad could be there for my big moment, too.

Samantha was holding hands with Sean, and when she saw me glance her way, she gave me a huge thumbs-up.

I could hardly believe I was the same Daisy Giordano. Me, friends with the Divine Devereaux? Homecoming queen? Dating Ryan Mendez? Even if a true clairvoyant had told me I'd be standing here, I probably wouldn't have believed it.

Despite my own psychic abilities, I couldn't predict how my future would turn out. And even though it was comforting to know where I stood, I thought as Ryan smiled at me and held my hand tightly, I realized I didn't have to know *everything*.

After all, Nightshade was a town chock-full of the unknown, the unusual, the unexpected. I adjusted my tiara and smiled and waved to the cheering crowd. Sometimes, something unexpected wasn't bad at all.

Acknowledgments

Thanks to my brilliant editor, Julie Tibbott. Who knew revision could be so much fun? Thanks to Nancy Russey, Connie Clark, Lori Polydoros, Shana Norris, and Emily Marshall, who answered my panicked pleas and gave me comments in record time. Thanks to Mary Pearson, Melissa Wyatt, Linda Johns, and Terry Miller Shannon for your friendship and wise counsel.

Thanks to the best in-laws in the world, Jim and Vera Perez. To Marissa, I know that you know that I'm not Gavin Rossdale. To Mikey, who drew football diagrams that I *almost* understood. To Michael, for everything.

Marlene Perez is the author of *Love in the Corner Pocket* and *Unexpected Development*, which was named an ALA Quick Pick for Reluctant Young Adult Readers. She lives in Orange County, California, where she's always on the lookout for vampires roaming her sunny suburb. So far, she hasn't spotted any.

www.marleneperez.com

Need more Nightshade?

Check out **DEAD IS A STATE OF MIND**, coming in January 2009!

Spring fever has taken over Nightshade, California. And when it comes to guys, the Giordano sisters sure know how to pick 'em: Rose is dating an undertaker. Poppy is dating a ghost. And Daisy is still with her longtime love, Ryan . . . or is she? Prom is only weeks away and Ryan still hasn't asked her to be his date.

But there's a gorgeous new guy at Nightshade High who has his eye on Daisy: Duke Sherrad, a fortune-teller claiming to have descended from Gypsies. Even though she's psychic herself, Daisy is skeptical of Duke's powers. But when a teacher who was the subject of one of his predictions ends up dead, she begins to wonder if Duke *is* the real deal after all.

Maybe if Daisy can track down the teacher's killer, she can find out the truth. The only trouble is, all signs point to the murderer being of the *furry* persuasion. Is Daisy any match for a werewolf? Maybe she is . . . in more ways than she bargained for!

Turn the page for a preview of **DEAD IS A STATE OF MIND**

CHAPTER ONE

I was running late. So late, in fact, that I didn't watch where I was going and slammed into someone walking out of the school office as I ran by.

"Ooph!" he said as my elbow jabbed into rock-hard abdominal muscles.

"I am so sorry!" I said. I'd almost knocked over a stranger. An extremely handsome stranger who stood there smiling at me, despite the fact that I'd almost flattened him in my hurry to get to chemistry class.

"Do not worry," he said with a heavy accent I couldn't place. "It is a pleasure to run into someone as beautiful as you on my first day."

He was dressed in a deep blue silk shirt, form-fitting black jeans, and boots. His spiky hair was really black, like someone had overturned an inkwell on his head. His long lashes framed incredible blue eyes.

"You're new here?" I said, stating the obvious. I knew

practically everybody at Nightshade High—and besides, it wasn't exactly swarming with gorgeous new students.

"I am Dukker Sherrad," he said, "but my friends call me Duke." He took my hand and held it longer than strictly necessary.

"Hi," I said.

He looked at me questioningly. I seemed to have forgotten my name as well as my manners.

"I'm Daisy Giordano," I finally said. I paused for a minute, waiting for recognition to set in, then felt like an idiot when my last name garnered only polite interest instead of the usual curiosity. You see, my mom is a psychic. She solves crimes all over the world using her powers. She wasn't exactly famous yet, but she'd been in the news plenty of times and I was getting used to people recognizing the name.

I blushed, amused at my overinflated sense of self-worth. "Welcome to Nightshade," I said.

Samantha Devereaux walked up as we stood there. She was blond, gorgeous, and the head cheerleader. She was also kind of a friend. Earlier in the school year, Sam had gone through a queen of the damned look, but that, thankfully, was over. She was wearing jeans I was sure would soon become all the rage and what looked like her boyfriend Sean's button-down shirt over a lacy camisole. It was outfits like this that earned her the nickname the Divine Devereaux.

I dropped Duke's hand. Quickly, but not quickly enough.

"Daisy, aren't you forgetting someone?" Samantha said pointedly. Remarks like this were why she was only kind of a friend. I thought *I* could be sarcastic, but I bowed before the master.

"What?" I was still staring into Duke's eyes, almost against my will.

"Ryan Mendez. Your boyfriend. He's waiting for you by your locker," she said.

Ryan. Oh my gosh! "I was supposed to meet him before class!" I said.

"I was hoping you would be available to show me around the school," Duke said.

"I've got to run," I said, "but this is Samantha Devereaux. I'll leave you in her capable hands."

As I left, Samantha said something to Duke I couldn't hear, and he laughed, dimples flashing. I felt a slight pang at leaving such a cutie behind, but another cutie waited for me.

I bolted to my locker, where Ryan was, as Samantha reported, waiting patiently.

"I'm so sorry!" I said. "I'm running late as usual."

Ryan leaned in for a quick kiss. "I don't mind waiting for you."

I smiled up at him. Maybe things between us were finally returning to normal. He'd been broody and distracted lately. He told me that he had been arguing with his dad a lot, which was odd since they had always been so close. I guessed it was because his dad could be strict at times — after all, he was the chief of police in Nightshade.

Broody or not, Ryan Mendez was the cutest boy in school (I pushed the memory of the gorgeous new guy out of my mind), played varsity in every sport the school had to offer, and was generally considered to be a catch by the girls at Nightshade High.

They also considered it a complete mystery that he wanted to be with me. I wasn't part of the popular crowd, although I'd been a cheerleader for about ten seconds back in the fall.

The warning bell rang, and we hurried to our classes. Ryan and I had P.E. together last period, but that was about it.

By fourth period everyone was gossiping about the new guy.

Penny Edwards was going full tilt when I walked into statistics class. Apparently, Duke was a foreign exchange student and was staying with her family, so she thought she was an expert on him. Who needed to call 4-1-1 when there was Penny?

"Duke Sherrad comes from a long line of gypsy fortune-tellers," she said importantly.

"Fortune-tellers?" I couldn't keep the incredulity from my voice.

"What's the matter, Daisy? The Giordanos can't handle a little competition?"

Did I mention that I'm psychic, too? But my abilities,

wonky at the best of times, don't hold a candle to my older sisters' talents. Rose's was mind reading and Poppy's was telekinesis. I can do both, just not very well.

Fortune-telling could mean that Duke had some sort of precognitive ability, if what Penny was saying was true, which was questionable. Penny talked first, asked questions later.

"Let's just say I'm a little skeptical," I said.

Penny barely disguised a sneer. "I think you're jealous," she said.

I opened my mouth, but the bell rang and Mr. Krayson started talking. "All right everybody, get out your books." He had an almost maniacal need for quiet in his classroom, and I wasn't going to test him.

A few minutes later, there was a knock at the door and Duke Sherrad came in. He handed a piece of paper to Mr. Krayson.

"I am very sorry to be late," Duke said. "I am not familiar with my classrooms as of yet."

"Please take a seat, Mr. Sherrad," Mr. Krayson said. He sounded positively affable, which was rare for him.

Penny gestured toward an empty seat near her, but Duke sat down next to me instead. Statistics was my least favorite subject and Mr. Krayson was my least favorite teacher, so the time crawled by. I spent the time counting the number of dirty looks Penny gave me. When class finally ended, I bolted out of the room.

"Daisy, please wait!"

I stopped and turned around. It was Duke. He hurried up to me, Penny at his heels.

"I had hoped you would show me to my next class," he said.

"I can show you," Penny said, but Duke sent me a pleading look. I took pity on him. Penny was a little much before lunch.

"What's your next class?" I said.

"Spanish," he said.

"I'm going there anyway," I said, ignoring Penny's fuming look. "I may as well show you."

"I am so grateful to you, Daizee," Duke said. His accent was even more noticeable now. He lifted my hand and pressed it to his lips just as we passed Ryan in the hallway.

I yanked my hand away and waved to Ryan. He waved back and gave me a quizzical look but kept going. He had Mr. Krayson next, so I knew he didn't have time to slow down, not without getting a tardy slip and a ten-minute lecture on punctuality.

I finally shook Duke off after Spanish class. I couldn't put my finger on why, but he was making me uneasy.

I dumped my books in my locker, and as I reached in to grab my lunch money, arms twined around my waist and pulled me against a hard body.

"Ryan, you scared the heck out of me!" I said.

"Who else would be grabbing you?" he said. "Is there something you want to tell me?"

"Of course not," I said. "I just wasn't expecting it."

He drew me closer and gave me a lingering kiss. "So who's your new admirer?" He said it casually, but I could feel his body tense.

"You mean Duke Sherrad?" I laughed like it was no big deal. Gorgeous or not, Duke didn't mean anything to me. Ryan did.

"I saw him kissing your hand in the hallway," Ryan said. His green eyes were intense.

"It was nothing," I said. I didn't mention anything about Duke sitting next to me in every class we shared.

"Good," he said. He leaned against the wall, pulled me close, and kissed me again. Several minutes later, he took a deep breath and said, "Are you hungry?"

"Starving," I admitted. "But by now there's probably nothing left at the cafeteria but cold tater tots."

"I planned ahead," he said, smiling triumphantly. He produced a picnic basket and tablecloth. "I thought we could have a picnic."

We went outside to find a shady spot on the lawn. A gaggle of girls had gathered around Duke Sherrad. Penny elbowed Alyssa when she tried to sit next to him.

Even Samantha was in his group. "Daisy, why don't you and Ryan come over here? Duke is telling our fortunes."

"Ryan packed a picnic," I said. "Thanks anyway."

"How about that spot over there?" I said. I pointed to a

spot as far away from Duke as possible without actually leaving the school grounds.

While Ryan unpacked the food, I stared at Duke. A fortune-teller, huh?

"You okay?" Ryan asked. He handed me a huge deli sandwich from Slim's Diner. My favorite restaurant.

"Fine," I said. I took a bite of my sandwich. "This was so sweet of you."

"I wanted to do something to make up for the way I've been acting lately," he said. "I know I haven't been the easiest guy to be around."

I took his hand. "It's okay."

"It isn't, but thanks for bearing with me," he said.

"Ryan, about prom—"

A piercing scream interrupted my words. Ryan and I leaped to our feet and ran toward the sound. Just another typical day at Nightshade High.